But Jamie had caught sight of something else. 'Alick,' he said. 'Look at that!'

On a table in the corner was a large black and gold chequered board, and on it was what seemed to be a chess set, but with bigger pieces than Alick had ever seen. And different. The black pieces were made of a dark stone. There were no pawns or bishops. Instead, as he noticed with a shock, there were three rows of hunched black birds with diamonds for eyes, each barb and feather accurately carved. Sightless, they glared at him.

The opposite pieces were the same size, but made out of what seemed like gold, and they glistened with emeralds and rubies and bright enamels. On this side were knights on horseback, ladies, minstrels with harps of jasper. Each was different, frozen in movement, their shields and surcoats blazing with colour; before them a row of greyhounds, cats and twisting serpents. Even the falconer was there, with his hooded hawk.

Jamie whistled. 'It's Them! Just like in the wood.'

The Conjuror's Game

Catherine Fisher

RED FOX

A Red Fox Book
Published by Random House Children's Books
20 Vauxhall Bridge Road, London SW1V 2SA

A division of Random House UK Ltd

London Melbourne Sydney Auckland
Johannesburg and agencies throughout the world

First published by The Bodley Head Children's Books 1990

Red Fox edition 1991
Reprinted 1991, 1992 (three times)

Printed and bound in Great Britain by
Cox & Wyman Ltd, Reading, Berkshire

ISBN 0 09 985960 2

To My Parents

Contents

'And as they looked they could hear a rider coming towards them, to the place where Arthur and Owein were over the gaming board. The squire greeted Arthur and said that Owein's ravens were slaying his bachelors and squires. And Arthur looked at Owein and said, "Call off thy ravens." "Lord," said Owein "play thy game." And they played. The rider returned towards the battle, and the ravens were no more called off than before.'

From 'The Dream of Rhonabwy' in the Mabinogion
(translated by Gwyn Jones and Thomas Jones)

1

The Brown Ointment

'There he is,' Mr Webster said.

'Who?'

'Luke Ferris. The chap I was telling you about. The conjuror.'

Alick stood up and had a look. Out in the street, on the opposite pavement, a thin, dark-haired man was looking in the shop windows. Just behind him trotted a white dog.

'Is that him?' Alick sat down again, and picked up the pen. 'I've seen him about before. He looks just like anybody else.'

'Ah, yes. I expect that's just what he wants you to think.' His father's mouth twitched. Alick knew something had amused him. 'Anyway, he's coming over, so you can find out for yourself.'

They watched the man cross the street, weaving between the cars. He came up to the window of Webster's Second-hand Bookshop and paused, looking in at the bright display of Christmas books and posters that Alick had spent the

1

morning arranging. Then the bell on the shop door jangled as he came in.

It was nearly five o'clock on a late December afternoon, and the shop was already quite dark. Down at one end, the fire had smouldered into embers, and the three shelves of musty, leatherbound books that never sold, gleamed in the warm glow. Mr Webster switched on the lamp near the window. 'Cold enough for snow, Luke,' he observed.

The conjuror nodded, and gave Alick a quick glance. His face was white with cold, and a gold earring glinted in the fire light. He wandered among the shelves, picking a book up now and again. Mr Webster searched the desk for his glasses, and Alick leaned his elbows on the counter and watched their customer.

A conjuror. And in Halcombe Great Wood that meant the real thing — not the man you saw on the television doing tricks with cards and white rabbits. And they said he was good. Well, he certainly looked at you in an odd way; as if he could see what you had for breakfast, if he wanted to. But *he* wouldn't be able to do anything about it either, Alick thought bitterly. No one could. The whole thing was hopeless.

A movement by the door caught his eye, and he saw that the white dog was lying there, watching him. Chin on paws it lay, and there was an odd smirk about its mouth, as if it found something funny.

The ashes of the fire crackled. The lights in the butcher's opposite went out. Finally, Mr Webster straightened up and slid the accounts book back to Alick with a satisfied nod. 'Good. All done.' He looked up.

'Anything you want, Luke?'

'Just these, I think.' The conjuror came and put two

books on the counter, and Alick took a sideways look at the titles. *The Medicinal Properties of Herbs and Simples* was the first, and the other was a small paperback called *Poisons*. He swallowed. Perhaps it would be better not to ask after all. But it was too late; as he wrapped the books his father had already begun.

'I'm glad you called in, Luke, I've been wanting a word for a while now. It's about Alick.'

'Oh?' Alick felt the man stare at him. 'What's he been up to?'

'Nothing.' Mr Webster laughed, pressing down a piece of sticky tape. 'No, it's his hands. Show him, Alick.'

Feeling foolish, Alick put both hands on the shop counter and stared at them gloomily.

Warts!

They looked horrible, and dirty, and they itched like mad. There were four on one hand and three on the other, including a big hard one like a knob of dried glue on the end of his thumb. He'd had them since he went fishing with Jamie in the Greenmere, but his father didn't know about that. The Mere was strictly out of bounds — a man had drowned in it last year. The kids at school had been calling him Frog-face ever since. He was just about sick of it.

The conjuror looked down at the warts thoughtfully. 'How long have you had these?'

'About three weeks.'

'And did they just appear?'

'Sort of,' Alick stammered.

'I see. You hadn't been anywhere wet? Mucky pools? Ponds?'

'No.'

Luke Ferris nodded. 'I see,' he said again. Suddenly he smiled at Alick; Alick felt himself go red. He knew!

'I've tried everything,' his father put in, pushing the parcel of books across the counter. 'Calamine, chilblain cream, every wart paint you've ever heard of. Then the doctor gave him some nasty, white burning stuff. None of it's done the slightest good . . . That'll be eight pounds fifty, please, Luke.'

'I think,' Luke said evenly, 'that I may be able to help. It'll cost you . . . eight pounds fifty. Payment on results.'

Mr Webster laughed. 'Fair enough.'

The conjuror gave Alick another grin, and reaching into his coat pocket, pulled out a few, small, round boxes which he scattered along the counter. Then he spread out a clean, white handkerchief and told Alick to put his hands on it, palms down. Warily, Alick obeyed. The warts itched like crazy. Mr Webster bolted the shop door, turned the sign to 'Closed' and came and leaned on the counter, filling his pipe and watching the proceedings with interest.

Humming, Luke opened one of the boxes. Immediately a sharp, pungent smell began to fill the shop, making Alick's eyes water. The dog by the door made a small noise in its throat.

'It's all right, Tam,' the conjuror said, without turning his head. Dipping one finger into the sticky, brown ointment, he carefully put a small dab of it on each of the warts, and two dabs on the large one, all the time humming and muttering words that Alick, close as he was, could not catch.

The smell made him feel dizzy, but the ointment did not sting as the doctor's had — it was just cold, like chocolate ice-cream. At last, the treatment seemed to be over; the shop was dim with a faint smoke. Luke wiped his finger clean on the edge of the handkerchief and replaced the box lid. He gathered the others up and dropped them in his

4

pocket. Alick watched the brown blobs of ointment harden into crusts. 'Can I move now?'

'Not yet. Let it dry.'

Impatient, he kept still. Luke and his father began to talk about people they knew, and he had to wait. The smell bothered him, made him think of deep woods and wet, mushy leaves. And he felt daft, with his hands out flat like someone at a seance.

'I hope it works,' he said when the talk had stopped.

Luke did not answer.

'It's horrible having people stare at your hands all the time.'

For some reason this seemed the wrong thing to say. His father glared at him angrily. He couldn't see why. But then the conjuror took his hands out of his pockets and laid them down flat beside Alick's.

'I know,' he said.

It was all Alick could do not to shout out. The long, brown hand next to his had, not five fingers, but *six*! He glanced at the other. It was the same.

Luke was watching him. 'Not so easy to cure as warts,' he said.

Alick felt foolish. 'I'm sorry,' he stammered. 'I didn't know.'

'I didn't think you did . . .' Luke paused, as if he was about to say something else, then, changing his mind, picked up the handkerchief and swiftly rubbed away the brown crusts from Alick's fingers.

Mr Webster gave a whistle of amazement.

The warts were gone. Just a crumble of fine dust lay on the counter.

Alick couldn't believe it. He stared at his fingers as if they did not belong to him, then touched them, carefully. No pain, no itching — not even a scar. Nothing!

Luke had already picked up his parcel of books and turned towards the door, nodding at Mr Webster's astonished thanks.

'Oh, that's all right. But if I were you, Alick,' he added, turning suddenly, 'I'd give up fishing at the Greenmere. It's not the sort of place you'll catch anything fit to eat. Besides, it's dangerous. Your father will tell you that.'

'Indeed I will,' Mr Webster said in a meaningful way.

The conjuror smiled. 'Goodnight, Tom.'

'Goodnight, Luke. Thanks again.'

And the door closed behind him.

Mr Webster turned around and took the pipe from his mouth, but before he could mention the Greenmere, Alick changed the subject.

'I never thought he could do it!' he announced, holding up his fingers to the light. 'It's magic!'

'It might look like that to you,' his father said, instantly sarcastic. 'Luke knows a lot about folk medicine and such. But it's true I've never seen warts done as fast as that, though there was an old chap down at Swinder's End used to do them, once. Didn't you feel anything?'

'No,' Alick plumped himself on to a stool. 'Dad, why didn't you tell me about his hands?'

'Well, I didn't know you'd come out with a tomfool remark like that, did I?' his father said. 'Besides, everyone knows. Or I thought they did. Odd, isn't it?'

Alick nodded.

'Mind, he's an odd sort is Luke.'

Alick clasped his knees. 'How do you mean?'

'Well, it's not just warts.' Mr Webster crossed to the fire

6

and began to rake it out. 'You know McCarthy, the baker? He had arthritis last year, very bad. The doctor told him he might be in bed for the rest of his life. Then his son called on Luke, and the next week the old man's in the Crown and Fiddle drinking pints. I'll bet he charged more than eight pounds fifty for that.' He straightened up and dusted his hands. 'Well now, I think we'd better go upstairs and have some tea, don't you? And a nice little chat. About the Greenmere.'

2

Greenmere

'And he did it just like that?' Jamie stared at Alick's hands. 'Get out! It's impossible!'

'It's not. Besides, Dad was there — ask him.' Alick was annoyed. 'You never believe anything I say.'

'Too much imagination,' Jamie said. 'It's all those batty old books, it is.'

'Oh shut up.' Alick felt guilty. He shouldn't be here, not after the row he had got last night. They were in the Combe, a narrow lane that ran deep into the wood; their heads bent against the bitter breeze. He pulled his gloves back on. 'It is true. And he does have six fingers. And what's more he knew I'd been at the Mere too.'

'Lucky guess.'

'No. He knew.' Alick kicked up the leaves. 'He said it was dangerous. And Dad knew then, of course.' He pulled a face.

'Was it bad?'

'Not really. Said I ought to think of other people.' And yet, he thought, here I am going there again.

Jamie must have guessed what he was thinking. 'Well, we're only going to walk past it. There's nothing wrong with that, is there? And I *must* have dropped that reel there; I've looked everywhere else.'

The Combe had been getting narrower for some time; now it was just a deep, gloomy cutting in the very lowest part of the wood. On each side, steep banks of earth towered over their heads, as if a knife had cut a deep slash in the ground and they stood at the bottom of it. In summer the banks were a riot of flowers, but now, in bleak December, only a tangle of tree-roots and frost-bitten brambles poked out of the soil. High above, crowding to the edge as if to look down, were rows of golden beech trees, their leaves filling the Combe in deep drifts to the boys' knees.

They climbed up by the usual way; a zig-zag staircase of roots that stuck out of one bank. At the top, the forest was silent all about them; a faint breeze rustled the tree-tops. Far down the ranks of trees a crow 'karked' noisily and flew away.

Briskly, Jamie started down the path. 'It's all nonsense, all this stuff about the Mere. I mean, I know that chap was drowned in it, but that's just because he fell in, or went swimming and got stuck. There must be acres of mud in there. You'd never catch me swimming in it!'

Behind him, Alick shook his head. 'That man had all his clothes on. You don't go swimming like that.'

'Well, he fell. It's just the same. But these yarns about the Mere being a bad place, and people who go into the wood and never come out again — that's just stuff! Stuff to keep little kids away from the edge.'

It sounded sensible. Jamie usually did — and he was always sure he was right. Alick said nothing.

'Are you listening?'

'Yes.'

'Good!' Jamie jumped on a fallen log and raced along it, arms wide. 'There's nothing here but rabbits, and squirrels, and birds, and, er . . .'

'Foxes,' Alick put in quietly.

'FOXES!'

The thin, red shape Alick had seen, loped off at the sudden shout. All at once they both burst into a fit of giggles, shoving and pushing each other and crashing noisily through the drifts of leaves.

Around them, echoes rang in the trees for miles.

Halcombe Great Wood stretches for fifty thousand acres, most of it rarely visited. Only four roads come into the Wood, meeting in a crooked X at Halcombe Cross. One of the lanes leads to Halcombe village; the other two are roads towards Gloucester and Monmouth; and the fourth, far more spindly and lost under its leaves, is the Combe, which goes only to the house at Swinder's End and then peters out in the trees. It is an ancient wood, a wildwood, riddled with lumps and humps, ruined cottages, and a maze of bridleways and tracks and paths.

Halcombe village is surrounded by trees. From the church tower, all you can see in any direction are endless dark green branches, and the cluster of red roofs like an island in the middle. And, if it is a fine day, you might see the sun glittering on the pinnacles of Gloucester Cathedral, thirty miles away.

You would also see Tolbury Tump. All the forest is hilly,

but Tolbury Tump stands out; a high round knoll, bare of trees, the only bald spot in the whole of the wood. And at the foot of the Tump, hidden in a gloomy hollow of dark pines, lies the Greenmere.

As Alick and Jamie trod the thick layer of pine needles towards it, their footsteps were muffled, and the reek of weed and rottenness seemed stronger than ever. Alick pulled a face. 'Yuk!'

The Mere stank. It was always green; a scum of algae lay on the surface like a heavy velvet cloth. It never seemed to break, either — even when you threw a stone in, it was just gulped down without a ripple, and there was no sign of that sudden opening and closing. It was a mouth; it swallowed things. No one in their right minds would go swimming in there.

The boys paused right at the edge.

'Now if I listened to you,' Jamie said slyly, 'I'd be waiting for some slimy hand to come out of that lot, grab me by the ankle, and haul me in.'

Alick laughed, but it wasn't funny. 'Forget the reel. Let's go up the hill,' he said. 'It's worse down here than usual, and darker.'

'Tut-tut. Scared of shadows.'

Alick ignored that. He looked at the trees. The leaves were black and heavy; glossy. Small bright lights glinted among them. He caught Jamie's sleeve.

'Look!' he whispered. 'In the branches!'

The trees were black with birds. Every twig, every branch, bent with their weight; a feathered host, a shadow of wings and beaks and bright eyes. Alick glanced from tree to tree. There were rows of them, sitting perfectly still, looking at him.

11

Jamie whistled. 'Crows. Where did they all come from?'

'Don't know.' Alick's eyes moved uneasily along the branches. 'Perhaps it's some kind of migration.'

'Crows don't, daft. It's weird.'

The breeze rustled. Black barbs of feathers rose and fell. Suddenly Alick turned. 'Let's go.'

'They're only birds.' Before Alick could stop him, Jamie picked up a handful of grit and flung it into the Mere with a tremendous splash. 'Go on,' he yelled, waving his arms. 'Clear off! Shoo!' But the birds did not move. Rank on rank they perched, hunched up in the wind.

Jamie backed away. When he spoke again his voice was quieter than usual. 'I don't get this. Let's get out of it.'

They turned, but Alick stopped so suddenly that Jamie slammed into the back of him. 'Hell!' he said.

Across the lake, sunlight was slanting into the trees, lighting up the wood. In the golden glade stood a line of horses, snorting and shifting, their pale manes lifting in the cold wind. One bent its long slender neck to the water, clinking its harness.

And on the golden horses, golden riders.

There were men with long cloaks and tunics to the knee, helmed, with spears slung at their saddles. There were women with long ropes of hair twisted with braid and gold thread; and minstrels with harps; grooms and huntsmen; falconers with their hooded hawks flapping and screeching on their wrists. Between the horses' legs, a pack of slim greyhounds twisted their leashes, growling and snuffling in the bushes.

'Mad,' Jamie muttered. 'That's it. I'm going mad.'

Alick shook his head. 'Then it must be both of us.'

Birds and horsemen eyed each other coldly.

12

'I'm not going to be scared of this lot.' Jamie thrust both fists into his pockets. 'Just walk slow. Back the way we came.'

'I don't think so.' Alick glanced back at the birds. 'Look at them. The way they're lined up. It's as if they're waiting for a battle. And we're in the middle.'

'Down here then.' Jamie pushed through the bushes at the edge of the Mere. 'We can get through.' The bank began to crumble gently at his feet.

'Be careful.'

'Oh, it's all right.'

Soil slipped and splashed into the water.

And then, in the wood, a horn rang out — an eerie, alarming, shattering of the stillness — and in answer, every bird in the trees opened its wings and screamed!

Jamie turned too quickly, slipped, flung out his arms. For a second he hung on the lip of the lake, then, with an enormous splash, he fell. The birds screeched; water cascaded over Alick's face.

'Jamie!'

The green carpet of the Mere was foaming and boiling. Hands and a face floundered and disappeared, bubbled up again, shouting. Desperate, Alick ran along the edge and yelled at the horsemen.

'He's drowning! For God's sake!'

Silent, unmoving, they stared at him. Their eyes were cold. One horse chewed grass, quietly.

Swearing, Alick tore off coat and boots and gloves. The water was ice round his knees; the mud of the Mere soft and cold around his feet. 'Swim!' he yelled. 'Keep up!' But the white face gasped and turned over and under, and without another thought he threw himself forward and the Mere opened its cold mouth and swallowed him.

13

After a black second he came up, gasping. The water was a solid weight on his clothes, pulling him down. He kicked towards Jamie; a dark commotion in the ripples somewhere ahead. Blue-lipped, breathless, he forced his arms and legs to move. They were lead weights, the effort to raise them exhausted him. The cold bit him; its teeth pierced through his fingers and bones and lungs. He grabbed at the dark heavy shape in the water, sank, swallowed green scum and vomited it out, caught a glimpse of pale sky far up over the trees.

Then the Mere put its hand over his mouth and dragged him down.

3

The Fidchell

Choking, kicking and struggling, Alick sank into blackness. But the hand held him; a thin, firm hand that heaved him up by his shirt, out of the sucking grip of the water, out into sudden wind and air and an explosion of roaring trees.

Luke dragged and shoved him to the bank. 'Get out,' he commanded. 'Hurry up.'

The birds and the horsemen were gone.

Confused, wet and gashed, Alick stumbled out on to the pine needles and slumped against a tree, gasping for breath in the bitter cold. The conjuror was waist-deep in the water; he had both arms under Jamie's shoulders and was half-dragging him to shore. Slowly they staggered out together and collapsed, breathless.

There was a moment of coughing and spitting and wiping of eyes.

Then Alick got his breath. 'We'd have drowned!' he yelled furiously.

'They wouldn't help . . . they just sat there!'

He pushed the wet hair out of his eyes and crouched down, shivering. The conjuror coughed, and the gold of his earring glinted. 'Who did?'

'The horsemen . . . those people . . . riders. And all those birds screaming at us . . .'

'Were they?' Luke looked at them both. 'Then you must have frightened them. Birds don't just scream at people.'

'Ordinary birds don't.' Jamie scraped green algae from his ears. 'These weren't ordinary. They were weird. Gosh, I'm frozen.'

He rubbed his face and arms furiously.

'It was as if they could think,' Alick said firmly. 'Not like birds at all. And who blew the horn? Who were those people?'

Luke stood up and tugged his wet shirt off, then picked up his coat from the floor and flung it on, shivering. Then he whistled. As the white dog came out from the trees, Alick said, 'You must have seen them.'

Luke did not answer. Angry now, Alick persisted. 'Jamie did.'

'Thought I did.'

'You know you did!'

Jamie laughed, despite the cold and the pain in his leg. 'Yes, all right. But I was too busy drowning.'

Alick turned to Luke. 'Did you see them?'

Luke shook his wet hair. 'I think you'd better come home with me. It's too cold to hang about.' And as if he had not heard, he hauled Jamie to his feet and started off with him through the wood.

Thoroughly annoyed, Alick trailed after them. They had seen those people, the horses, the strange gold colour of their clothes. What's more, Luke had seen them too. He must have. So what was going on?

Talley was a small woodman's cottage, among the trees on the north side of Tolbury Tump. It was quite isolated, and only a narrow, overgrown track led down to it from the main road. By the time they reached the house, they were all shaking uncontrollably with the cold, and Alick's clothes stuck to him, wet and stiff with the smelly algae. He was very relieved to see smoke rising from the chimney.

Luke lifted the latch and hurried them in. While they huddled numbly over the fire, he dragged out some dry logs and tossed them on, stirring the blaze up rapidly; then disappeared into the kitchen. A few minutes later he came back with a huge bowl of steaming water and some dark blue towels.

'Here. Get the worst off — and those wet clothes. I'll see if I've got anything you can wear.'

It was glorious to feel the hot water on their faces and bodies after the icy wind. They got as much of the green scum off as they could, then spread their clothes to dry and sat huddled up in towels next to the blaze. Jamie's ankle was swelling fast. He touched it, gingerly.

'Ouch.'

'Does it hurt?'

'Like hell. My throat is stinging too. I swallowed pints of that muck.'

'And me.' With the stinging of his hands and face, Alick had forgotten his annoyance. 'It'll be a wonder if we're not poisoned.'

'We'll catch something worse at home, anyway. Or I will.' Jamie sighed and wriggled his toes. 'I can just about feel my feet now. Funny sort of place this, isn't it?'

Alick nodded. It was a small, dark room with scraps of rug on the floor and bare rafters above. There was only one window, and the light that filtered in was dim and green from the trees outside. A dresser stood at one end; its shelves and drawers crammed with boxes and jars, dirty dishes, papers, shells, stones, books. Bunches of herbs hung from the ceiling; some were so crisp that their leaves had dropped off and lay crushed on the floor. The window-sill was jammed with dusty books, and muddy wellingtons and a spade leaned by the door. Around the walls hung branches of holly and mistletoe, and a white cat walked along the back of Jamie's chair. It was all rather untidy, but warm and comfortable. Alick liked it.

But Jamie had caught sight of something else. 'Alick,' he said. 'Look at that!'

On a table in the corner was a large black and gold chequered board, and on it was what seemed to be a chess set, but with bigger pieces than Alick had ever seen. And different. The black pieces were made of a dark stone. There were no pawns or bishops. Instead, as he noticed with a shock, there were three rows of hunched black birds with diamonds for eyes, each barb and feather accurately carved. Sightless, they glared at him.

The opposite pieces were the same size, but made out of what seemed like gold, and they glistened with emeralds and rubies and bright enamels. On this side were knights on horseback, ladies, minstrels with harps of jasper. Each was different, frozen in movement, their shields and surcoats blazing with colour; before them a row of greyhounds, cats and twisting serpents. Even the falconer was there, with his hooded hawk.

Jamie whistled. 'It's Them! Just like in the wood. And

18

they must be worth a *fortune*! Real gold, I'll bet . . .'

'They can't be.' Alick stood up, gathered his towel about him, and padded over to the table. He picked up one of the horsemen. 'Gosh, it's heavy though.' Thoughtfully he put it down, and picked up something else. 'I wonder what this is for?'

It was a piece that stood by itself in the middle of the board. A golden tree. Tiny leaves of metal hung from it, and made a quiet, tinkling noise as he raised it. The leaves nearest the gold army were gold, and those on the other side, nearest the black army of birds, were black. He turned it round, and gasped.

'What's up?' Jamie could only see his friend's back.

'Nothing.' Alick stood very still. How could he say what he had seen — that as he had turned the tree, the black leaves were now gold and the gold, black! Was it a trick of the light? No . . . there it was again. No matter how much you turned it round, the gold leaves were always by the gold pieces. 'Come and look at this,' he began, but a growl silenced him.

Luke's dog had come into the room. It growled again, teeth bared.

'Better put it down,' Jamie muttered.

Nervously, Alick's hand moved an inch towards the board. An explosion of barks nearly made him drop the piece.

'Tam! That's enough!'

The conjuror raced down the stairs, pushed the dog aside, then came and took the tree swiftly out of Alick's hand. His six fingers closed around it, tight.

He gave Alick a peculiar look. 'Like it, do you?'

'Yes . . . I was just looking . . .' Alick could feel himself going red. 'It's not chess, is it?'

'Fidchell,' the conjuror said, putting the tree gently back on its central square. 'A very old game. Not played much now.'

And then someone laughed.

Alick looked round, astonished. It hadn't been Luke, or Jamie. The room was dark; there was no one else in it but the dog, watching him with that same smirk it had had in the shop.

'What was that?' Jamie asked.

'Owls. You hear them all the time.' Luke tossed a bundle of clothes carelessly towards them. 'Here, try these. They'll be a bit big, but they're all I've got.'

While they were dressing and giggling at the rolled-up trousers and large shirts, he stood leaning against the table, watching them. Alick felt uneasy. Surely Luke didn't think he'd have stolen that tree? And how were the pieces the same as those people . . . and the birds?

When they were dressed, Luke laughed at them, and strapped Jamie's ankle with a tight, white bandage and some stuff to stop it hurting. Then he gave them a hot drink that wasn't tea or coffee, but whatever it was it drove the cold right out, and Alick suddenly felt warm and glowing to his finger-ends.

While they were drinking it, Luke went out, and when he came back he said he had been down to the telephone box on the road and phoned Jamie's father. 'He'll be here in about five minutes.'

'Thanks. I'd never walk it.'

'Where's the dog?' Alick asked, glancing round.

'Outside.'

Alick was glad. He didn't like it. He kept thinking it was the thing that had laughed.

There was silence for a while. Alick stroked the cat. Jamie was moving his ankle, testing it. Alick noticed Luke's eyes move across the room, from door to stairs, as if he was watching someone cross the room. There was nothing there. Then, upstairs, a door slammed.

At the same time, the conjuror leaned forwards and poked the fire. 'Didn't I tell you yesterday not to go near the Mere?'

Alick was tongue-tied.

'It was my fault.' Jamie put in. 'I lost a reel. Still haven't found it either.'

Luke made no comment. Instead, he said, 'The Mere is a bad spot. There are places like that — places that have a bad effect on animals, and birds, even people. I suppose you do physics at school?'

They nodded.

'Well, there are physical causes for it,' Luke went on, staring into the fire. 'It may be something to do with magnetic forces in the earth. They affect people's nerves, make them ill, uneasy. The Chinese have a science called feng shui — it means they find out these places and then they keep away from them. I advise you to do the same.'

Something's going on, Alick thought. Something queer, that he doesn't want us to know about.

The fire made a row of strange shadows walk down the wall.

'But you live here,' Jamie objected.

'I do.' The conjuror gave him a look that wiped the grin off his face. 'But I'm different.'

Alick glanced at the hands holding the poker. He must have seen them, those riders and those birds — gold and black, like the Fidchell.

21

But the purr of a car up the track interrupted him. Luke got up abruptly and went to the door. 'It's your father, Jamie. Come on.'

4

The Hollow Hill

When Alick walked into the bookshop ten minutes later, Mr Webster nearly fell off his stool with laughter. 'Where on earth did you get those clothes! Oxfam?'

Alick scowled. 'They're not mine. I fell . . . well, I got wet. In a stream. Your friend Luke lent me these.' And he hauled himself up on the counter and told his father about the strange riders, and the black birds, and Luke, but took care not to mention the Greenmere.

'Talley, eh? I've never been inside,' his father said curiously, filling his pipe. 'What's it like?'

'Scruffy. All right though. All sorts of odd things. That reminds me, how do you play Fidchell?'

'What?'

'Fidchell.'

'Never heard of it.'

'It's a game,' Alick explained. 'Like chess. Luke's got a set. Jamie thought some of the pieces were gold.'

'Gold!' Mr Webster snorted as he put the bolt across the door. 'Oh, I'm sure. I suppose you want a set for Christmas? Gold, my eye!'

While his father laughed and smoked and struggled with the accounts, Alick ran upstairs and changed. He put his wet clothes in the bottom of the basket in the bathroom, hoping his father wouldn't find them. Then he came downstairs and went along the 'Natural History' shelf until he found a good bird book. That was one advantage of living in a bookshop — you had your own library.

He looked up crows. The picture showed two black, rather scruffy birds, but they weren't right. But on the next page was a raven — big, hunched, with a beak like a nutcracker. That was it, ravens. Not crows. But according to the book they were very rare. It was odd. The whole business was odd.

He put it back and looked for something on Fidchell. It was that tree that had fascinated him: he couldn't forget the way the leaves had changed. But none of the books made any mention of the game at all, until finally, in a battered old encyclopaedia without a cover, 50p in the bargain box, he found this:

FIDCHELL (or WOODEN WISDOM)

A board game, probably similar to chess, consisting of two armies of men on a chequered board. Known to have been played by the Celts, this game is mentioned in several ancient texts, and is known to have had magical meaning. No known pieces have been found. The rules are nowhere recorded. Pronunciation: *Fee*-kell.

Puzzled, he asked, 'Dad, how long ago were the Celts?'

'Oh, hundreds of years,' his father said absently. 'Before

24

the Romans. Now don't start reading down here. We're closing.'

Hundred of years. No pieces found. It didn't make sense. Even more puzzled, he put the book back in the box, then took it out.

'Can I keep this?'

'If you want. 50p.'

Jamie telephoned that night. 'My ankle's the size of a balloon,' he moaned. 'Stay off it till Christmas, the doctor says. *And* I'm having a bike! What's the use if I can't ride it?'

Alick laughed.

'Shut up, heartless. Listen, that Luke character is *weird*!'

'Well, I told you, didn't I!'

'Ah, but I still don't swallow all that about the warts. But those chess pieces, that was uncanny . . .'

Alick nodded. 'He saw them too . . . in the wood, whatever he said. I know he did.'

'Yes. And that means you'll have to find out what's afoot, my trusty sidekick.'

'Me?'

'Well, I can't, can I?' Jamie demanded. 'It's easy. Just watch him. Follow him. Use your brain.' He giggled, 'What there is of it.'

It was when he was crouched behind a tree outside Luke's cottage, and trying to edge his cramped feet into an easier position, that Alick realized that finding things out was cold, uncomfortable and, up to now, boring.

He ate his last-but-one bit of chocolate, and counted the chimes from Halcombe church as they rang out over the tree-tops. Five o'clock. He'd been there an hour already. Around him the forest was dark and silent; far off in the trees, a patch of moonlight showed. And it was getting colder. He thought about his supper, hot in the oven.

Then, the light in Luke's window went out; a figure came down the path, opened the gate, and moved off among the trees. Alick slipped after him, without a sound. Whatever Luke knew, he would find it out.

The moon striped the wood black and silver like a great badger. Far down the path, Luke's figure glimmered across a patch of light and vanished into darkness again. There was no sign of the dog — which was just as well, Alick thought.

He tried to get a bit closer. It was hard to see in the dappled wood, and if Luke left the path he might miss him altogether. The conjuror was a flicker of movement ahead; he seemed to be heading straight for Tolbury Tump.

Once he was sure of this, Alick could concentrate on keeping quiet. He had cracked two twigs already, and once, Luke had looked back as if he had heard something. Flattened against a beech bole, fingers gripping the smooth cold sides, Alick watched the conjuror turn and walk on. He was more careful after that.

A few minutes later he had a shock. It was starting to snow. Tiny grains floated in the air like scraps of paper; his breath smoked as he walked. By the time they reached the bottom of the Tump and had begun to climb, there was a fine powder underfoot, crunching as he stepped on it. Luke went up the hill and Alick, back in the shadows, wondered why. The path was steeper now, twisting through tree-roots and old rabbit burrows. Finally, he came to the very edge of the trees and looked out.

The top of Tolbury Tump was a grey dome, gleaming faintly with snow. Under the precise silver ring of the moon, Luke was walking up the slope. He came to a small hollow in the hillside, where a few scrubby bushes clung out of the wind, and stopped. He looked around, cautiously. Then he turned aside and went down into the hollow.

There was a ditch along the wood's edge. Alick jumped down into it and squirmed along until he could see between the bushes. Snow swirled in his eyes. Between the flakes he saw Luke stoop. There was a noise. He listened, intently.

Tap. Tap. Tap.

The knock of stone on stone.

More snow. He wiped his eyes. What was Luke doing? and *what was that!*

It was light; bright and golden. As he stared, a great slot of light was swinging slowly open in the hillside, reddening his face and making the falling snow glitter like golden grains.

Then the conjuror stepped inside, and with a click the door was shut.

In the cold moonlight, Alick's breath made a slow cloud. He took the last piece of chocolate from his pocket and ate it, automatically, tasting nothing. Then he crinkled the silver paper. Ideas were flooding into his head. Tugging his feet out of the mud, he watched the moon as, agonizingly slowly, the cloud drifted over it. Now it was a dome, now a fingernail, now a faint line closing up at the edges. As soon as it was gone, he leapt up, ran up the slope and jumped into the hollow. Brambles whipped round him; the hole was full of thorns and scrubby rowan; a steep earth cliff overhung it. The snow was settling, but he groped round till he found a stone, and then crouched down by the one big grey boulder. Brushing the snow away he pulled a glove off and felt the surface: spirals and circles, old zig-zag lines. Then he raised the stone as Luke had done, and knocked.

Tap. Tap. Tap.

The light caught him before he could move; a dazzling slit, widening in the hollow, reddening rowan berries to globes of fire.

Crouching, he turned to face it.

Behind him a small door stood open in the hillside; the light shone out of it. He saw a long tunnel. The walls gave out the light; they glimmered golden, and hundreds of thin, golden pinnacles and pillars upheld the roof. They were not smooth, but twisted and spindly like young trees. Their roots spread over the floor, and they even had stony branches — nets of fruit and leaves on the cavern roof. There was no sign of Luke. Far ahead the tunnel turned a corner.

Alick stood up, bit his lip, and stepped inside.

5

First Move

He was standing in pitch darkness.

Alick swore in surprise; he hadn't even heard the door shut. Carefully he stretched out his hands into emptiness. Then he moved — and crack! his head hit something so hard, the tears jerked into his eyes.

'Damn!' he hissed, clutching his head in both hands. It was the ceiling. It felt cold and knobbly through his gloves. It shouldn't have been so low. Hurriedly, he felt in his pocket, found a box with three matches in, and struck one. Then, shielding the glow, he gazed around.

Slabs of grey stone, and a litter of bones and rubble on the floor. No sign of a door. There were spirals and squiggles carved on the rocks, like the boulder outside. Then the match scorched his fingers. He threw it down, bewildered. Where were the golden pillars? And where was Luke?

'Luke?' he whispered.

Echoes whispered back. He began to move, cautiously. It

was difficult, shuffling a few inches at a time, trying not to make any noise on the loose stones, and keeping one hand on the clammy, invisible wall. As he went deeper into the hill it got colder, and the air grew earthy and unpleasant. Then he stopped.

He could hear voices.

They were low, and far ahead, but they were there.

He went on, carefully, and at each twist of the tunnel the murmuring grew louder, until it sounded like a few men talking quietly. One of them must be Luke. Then Alick realized he could see his hand, and the tunnel wall. And round the next bend the tunnel ended.

It was closed by a glimmering, golden curtain that fell to the floor. His hand reached out to it, and had almost touched it, when a sudden uproar of laughing and clapping froze him with terror, his heart thumping loudly and his hands clenched in his gloves.

But no one came through, and the talk went on. Music was playing too; low, subtle and strange, it drew him to the curtain — he could see a few blurred forms through it; the glow and crackle of a fire. He heard chairs being pushed back, and somewhere a door opening and closing. A smell of flowers, an impossible summery smell, wafted out.

Then there was silence.

He waited a few minutes, then carefully reached out and pulled a corner of the curtain aside.

A large hall lay before him, with a fire burning in its centre — the flames were sweet smelling and strangely smokeless. The walls were golden, the floor, chequered with huge squares of black and gold, and the same pillars he had seen in the tunnel held up the roof — their trunks twisted like ice, tinkling with frosty fruits and leaves.

Alick stepped further into the hall. At the far end, he saw three doors, all closed, and in front of them, near the fire, were two chairs facing each other across a small table. There was nothing else.

He padded across the cold floor, feeling snow drip from his shoulders. The table had a board on it. The Fidchell pieces stood there, gleaming gold and black in the firelight.

He was beyond surprise; anything could happen now. Carefully he picked up the tree and turned it. Just as he'd thought — the leaves changed colour. It was inexplicable . . . magical.

Suddenly he noticed something lying on the floor by one of the chairs. It was a fruit, like a cherry, but pure white. He picked it up and smelled it; felt its soft juiciness under his fingers, imagined its sweetness. The next minute he had eaten it.

He knew at once it was a mistake. There was no delicious taste, it was just like water in his mouth — rather sour water too. It made him feel sick. The room looked different, shadowy, in the corners, and he felt dizzy, like the time he had drunk a whole tumbler of his father's port. And there must be something wrong with his eyes, because the Fidchell pieces had all turned their heads and were looking at him; the knights amused, the ladies laughing, the dogs and horses shifting, the black birds in ominous silence. He backed towards the curtain, watching one raven unfurl its wings and stare.

The curtain was a rag of cobweb. He tore it down and plunged into the tunnel, banging and bumping himself in the darkness as the noise rang around him; laughter, low and mocking, cat-calls, whistles, the beat of wings. He ran so fast and so carelessly that he had crashed into the smooth

31

surface of the door before he realized, and it swung open without a sound, spilling him out into the bitter cold of the hollow. Breathless, he crouched, and looked back.

In the distance, down the tunnel, shadows moved. Black, golden, they flickered towards him. He flung himself on the door and heaved, but it stayed open, unmoving — the golden light bathing the rowan bushes — and when the first horn rang faintly in the distance, he turned and fled, leaving it wide.

He crashed to the lip of the hollow, took a deep breath, and let it out in amazement. He had forgotten the snow! The hillside was a white sheet; the air full of flying patches that muffled the moon. Reckless, he jumped knee-deep into the drifts and struggled for the wood.

Noise pursuing him, he raced along the path, coughing and spluttering. Snow stuck to his hair and eyelashes, branches tripped him; he was sure that his noisy crashing run could be heard for miles. And perhaps he was half a mile down the path before he realized what he had in his hand.

Small and enigmatic, the tree from the Fidchell board shimmered and tinkled. Without stopping, he stared at it, taking in the truth. What an idiot he was! But it was too late to worry about that now. He shoved it into the pocket of his coat, and ran all the faster.

Even so, after ten more minutes he had to slow down, clutching his aching side. He was so breathless and dizzy he hardly recognized where he was before the earth fell away suddenly in front of his feet, and below him the Combe lay silent and leaf-littered in the moonlight.

He slipped and slid and slithered to the bottom. Only then, when the sudden silence fell, did he look up. High overhead, crowding among the trees, a host of shapes gazed down at him. He saw glints of metal and gold; horses and men. And in the branches, the birds.

He said nothing. The horses clinked their harnesses; the rows of eyes did not move from him. Both sides were there, and he knew they wanted that tree. That damned tree.

It was about a mile to the village — it might just as well be ten, he thought, bitterly. He tried a step forward and nothing happened. He took another, then yelled in fright and leapt back.

The spear quivered in the leaves by his foot. There was no sign who had thrown it; the dark ranks were silent and unmoving.

Alick rolled his hands into fists. 'Listen!' he shouted, and then stopped, ears catching that new, deep purr behind him. A car!

But the listeners had heard it, too. With a cry and a hiss the thin sinuous shapes of hounds and serpents poured over the lip of the hollow. Alick turned and raced along the lane, waving and shouting as the humming in the air grew. Something grabbed his coat, wrapping round his ankle; in a flurry of leaves he fought and kicked and struggled.

'Alick? Alick Webster?'

Bewildered, he opened his eyes. Snowflakes swirled in the glare of two large headlamps. Someone was leaning out of the car.

'It is you, isn't it? Have you hurt yourself?'

'Er, no. Thanks.' Alick climbed stiffly to his feet and glanced around. The Combe was empty.

'Going home? Hop in then.'

The passenger door jerked open, and Alick slid hastily in and slammed it tight. The warmth of the car, its smell of

33

tobacco and leather, wrapped him like a blanket. The driver switched on the light.

'Hello, Vicar.'

'You're a bit wet,' the vicar remarked, releasing the brake. Alick realized that water was dripping all over the seat.

'Sorry. It's snow.'

'That's all right. Just take your coat off and put it in the back. On top of that big box will do. It's just stuff for decorating the church. That's better.'

It was. Alick felt the warmth prickle his hands and cheeks. The snow had soaked his trousers though, and the tips of his ears ached.

The car droned up the Combe in a flurry of snow. He gazed out of the window, but only saw himself and some flying branches.

'Coming to the Carol Service?'

'Yes . . . probably.'

'Good, good. That's what all those boxes are for, to decorate the little chapel at Ashton Bailey – It'll be there this year as usual – though the place is so old and damp, I wonder how the Lord keeps it up. You've seen the old tombs there? Mind if I drop you here?'

Alick nodded. The street lamps were on in Halcombe, and the bookshop window was bright with red and gold. As they pulled in, the vicar asked, 'How's the coin collection?'

'Oh fine, thanks.'

'You don't want any old halfpennies, do you?'

Alick shrugged. 'If you've got any rare ones . . .'

'Oh, I don't know the dates,' the vicar laughed, fishing Alick's coat out of a box. 'Just found a bag of them in a cupboard. Come and get them sometime. You never know, they might be worth something.'

34

The light was on over the bookshop. As Alick waited for his father to open the door, he wondered what time it was. And he was half-way up the stairs when he realized the pockets of his coat were empty. He had lost the little tree.

6

Inquisition

'Six ninety-five, please.' Alick pushed the book across the counter and then dropped the money in the till.

'Merry Christmas,' the woman said cheerfully.

Then the shop was empty, the first time that morning. He went over and poked the fire, and fetched more coal. Then he noticed one of the decorations had fallen down, and pinned it up with a drawing pin still bent from last year. Still no customers. He went to the window.

Halcombe High Street was full of shoppers slipping on the snow. Outside most shops it had been scraped away, but some still lay outside the houses and the empty shop, trodden down flat like dirty marzipan. A lorry was gritting the road, and the butcher was putting up a sash saying 'We wish all our Customers the Compliments of the Season.' Alick was wondering what they were, when the shop door opened with a loud jangle and Luke Ferris walked in, glanced around, and flipped the sign over to say 'Closed' in one deft movement.

'Hey! You can't do that!'

'Can't I!' The conjuror's eyes were black and he did not smile. The dog padded to the fire. Luke followed it and warmed his hands.

'Was it you?'

Alick was nervous. 'Was what me?'

'You know very well.'

Alick reddened. 'The shop's open,' he stammered, going to the door and changing the sign. 'Do you want to buy something?'

Luke drew himself up and leaned on the mantelpiece. But just then a young woman with a baby came in and asked Alick for books on Italian cookery. He tried to be polite, showing her the shelf and taking out books, and all the time watching the conjuror from the corner of his eye. Luke did not seem to move, but after a few minutes something changed in the shop. It was mustier, dimmer. Alick counted the girl's change for the third time — the coins seeming to multiply and slither from his suddenly clumsy hands. She smiled, gave him back a pound, and went to the door. The cold draught swirled the strange blue sparks in the fire to a glittering fountain. It was hard to breathe. He leaned on the counter, sleepily.

After a moment, Luke went to the door, locked it, turned the sign, and pulled the blind down on the window. Then he pushed Alick into a chair.

'Can you hear me?' he asked coldly.

Alick nodded. The voice came from a dark blurr standing over him.

'Tell me how you got into the hill.'

'. . . I . . . followed you,' he mumbled.

'Me!' Luke crouched down and clutched the chair arm. 'Last night?'

37

Somebody tried the door handle. Luke ignored it.

'What did you see?'

Alick didn't answer.

'Tell me!'

'Chairs. A table. A game like yours. And three doors.'

'Did you open any of the doors?' the voice asked softly.

'No.'

'But you took the tree, didn't you?'

Alick nodded, miserable. It was easier to breathe now. His sight was clearing. 'I didn't mean to. I didn't know till later. I suppose I got scared; starting to think those . . . things were after me.'

Luke was watching him carefully. 'So you ate something too. You've been very stupid, Alick. It's a long time since the Fidchell was played. And it's no game.' He drummed his fingers on the table. 'Go and get the tree. We might still have time.'

Alick felt sick. 'I've lost it,' he said.

Luke was silent for at least a minute.

Suddenly scared, Alick tried to explain. 'It might have been in the Combe . . . or in the vicar's car — it must have fallen out of my pocket. Is it . . . that important?'

Luke laughed, harshly. 'Important!' For a moment he seemed lost for words. Then he straightened. 'Alick, by taking the tree you've started the game. Both armies — the Black and the Gold — will be after it, anywhere, wherever it is. They'll spill out into the wood, into the villages, searching, hunting, letting nothing stand in their way.' He stared at the fire. 'Last time it happened here was in 1561.'

'The Black Winter?'

Luke nodded. 'Blizzards, famine, trees falling, un-explained migrations of animals, flooding. Fires, that started for no reason. Dead men, found in ditches. Portents and strange signs in the sky. That's the Fidchell, Alick. And now you've started it again.'

For a moment they were both silent. Then Luke sighed, rummaged in his pockets and brought out a small wax candle, pale green and about an inch high. 'We must find it, that's all. Have you got a mirror?'

'Upstairs.'

'Get it. Tam, go with him.'

The white dog raced up the stairs before Alick. Then it went into the bathroom, jumped on to the bath, and stared into his father's shaving mirror.

'Get down!' Alick snapped — then stared. For a moment he had seen a different face in the glass. A pale, thin, laughing, dangerous face. Then it was just the dog, ears pricked.

He took the mirror downstairs, thoughtfully.

'Your dog's one of them, isn't he?'

Luke laughed. 'What dog?'

A small white cat lay by the fire, washing.

Luke lit the candle and put it in the middle of the mirror. It had an unpleasant smell.

'This may help us,' Luke said. 'Don't speak, and don't touch the mirror.' Then, muttering something, he picked up the candle and poured the hot wax on to the glass.

The small pool was almost white; faint smoke came from it. Alick expected it to go hard, but it didn't. Bubbling and hissing, the film spread. Then he saw things come into it. First, dark, meaningless quivers, then a house, a tree, moonlight glinting on some water. Luke was staring at it, waiting.

Suddenly, the picture changed. Faint and grey as a

cobweb, he saw a stone figure of a man, lying on its back. The man's legs were crossed at the ankles. His face was covered in dust. A spider ran over his chest, and a dead leaf gusted by. Then the wax was white and cold and smooth.

'It looked like a tomb.'

'Yes,' Luke said quietly. 'And I think I know where:'

The doorhandle rattled. A loud knocking startled them. 'Alick! Open up!'

'It's my father,' Alick said, but Luke pushed him back. 'Wait. Be at my house this afternoon. Two o'clock. Right?'

Alick nodded. 'Yes, but . . .'

The letterbox rattled. 'Alick!'

'Just be there,' Luke went on, shoving the candle into his pocket. 'We've got to sort this thing out.'

'ALICK!'

'Coming!' he yelled, opening the door. Cold bright air struck his face.

'Give us a hand, then.' Mr Webster began to tug in a few heavy boxes. 'It's damn cold out here!' He stalked to the fire. 'And the shop shouldn't be shut yet, and it's as smoky as . . . Oh, hello, Luke.'

'Tom,' said the conjuror, thrusting his hands in his pockets.

'Tam Lin, too.'

'Yes, we just dropped in.'

'His warts haven't come back, you know.'

'They won't.' Luke called the dog and went to the door. 'Merry Christmas to you both.' And with a meaningful glance at Alick, he went out and walked swiftly up the snowy street.

Alick watched him go. 'He's a daunting sort of person, isn't he? Always seems to know much more than you do.'

'Very,' said Mr Webster. 'Alick, isn't this my shaving mirror? And what's this muck all over it?'

7

The Hosting

At ten to twelve, Jamie phoned.

'Listen, Sunshine,' said the testy voice, 'how about visiting a poor invalid? I still exist you know. It's not the Black Death.'

Alick grinned. 'How's the foot?'

'Sore. Why didn't your magician friend give me some magical cure?'

'Perhaps he thought you deserved it.'

'Found anything out?'

Alick thought about it. 'Not really,' he said. 'And if I do, I'll tell you.' He knew just how much Jamie would believe of all this. Nothing.

'That reminds me,' Jamie said. 'Those birds were ravens. Did you hear it on the radio?'

'No. What?'

'About the ravens. A bird-watching chap was talking about them. All sorts of reports they'd had, of these huge black birds. Ouch, my cat's walking on my leg!'

Alick laughed, and promised to go over the next day — Christmas Eve. Then he went thoughtfully back into the sitting-room.

His father was sitting by the fire. Large boxes of books were piled by his feet; he was writing prices on the front pages.

'1878,' he remarked. 'First Edition. Very good. Might get fifteen pounds for that. Your dinner's hot, and I got you one of those ghastly sticky things you like, from Thomas's.'

'Good.' Alick sat at the table, picked up his fork and switched the radio on.

'Today has seen the worst blizzard conditions in the west of England for sixteen years,' said a woman's voice briskly. 'Four feet of snow fell overnight in some parts. Roads in the Mendips and Cotswolds are impassable, and helicopters from nearby RAF Arlington have been dropping supplies and fodder to outlying farms . . .'

'Oh, very nice,' Mr Webster muttered. 'Look, Alick, if it's too bad for me to get back tonight, lock up and go to Jamie's, all right?'

Alick nodded. He had forgotten his father was going to the book fair.

'And finally, on a lighter note,' the announcer continued, 'at Halcombe Great Wood, in Gloucestershire, several curious phenomena have been reported. Flocks of large, unidentified birds have invaded farmers' fields, and residents claim to have seen packs of spectral hounds and riders streaming across the sky.'

'Ha!' Mr Webster grinned. 'After closing time!'

Alick said nothing. It's all starting, he thought. He felt rather cold.

'Oh, I saw 'em all right,' said a loud local voice. 'Great

white cloudy things, like dogs, like, and horses. Tops of the trees all cracking under them. Streaming down from the Tump they were, and the whole of the wood shaking, and full of wind, and noise . . .'

Mr Webster stared at the radio. 'Sounds like Jacky Harris. I thought he was teetotal.' He poked the fire. 'Well, well. Seen any spectral hounds, Alick?'

'I thought I saw one,' Alick said thoughtfully. 'In your shaving mirror.'

On the way to Luke's he had to pass the vicarage, and on a sudden impulse he knocked at the door. He could have dropped the tree in the car; it would be easy enough to find out.

The door opened with a jerk; the housekeeper glared out. When she saw Alick, her frown cleared. 'Oh, sorry, love. We've had a few queer callers round here this morning.'

She left him in a big room with lots of bookshelves and potted plants. A clock ticked in one corner. Alick sat on the edge of the settee and twisted his scarf, nervously. Out in the snowy graveyard a black bird landed on a tombstone. He looked at it suspiciously. Was it one of *Them*?

The door opened.

'Alick!' the vicar said, dumping a pile of books on the piano. 'I thought it might be you. Now let me see, where did I put it . . .'

For a glorious moment, Alick thought he meant the tree, but the vicar dumped a small plastic bag on to the table. Coins spilled and rattled and rolled.

'There. Anything interesting?'

Alick swallowed his disappointment and sorted through the coins. 'The Maundy sixpence is nice — early, and

44

almost mint, too. Most of the halfpennies I've got . . . um, and halfcrowns. None of it's worth much, I'm afraid.'

'Never mind,' said the vicar. He smiled nostalgically as Alick gathered up the coins. 'Used to collect moths myself, at one time. Had to stop though; takes up too much room — all those cabinets and boxes. Display yours, do you?'

Alick nodded. 'I've got a room upstairs.'

'Ah! Big old house.'

Alick buttoned his coat slowly. 'Um, there was one thing I wanted to ask. I think I may have dropped something in your car. A little tree . . . a piece from a game.'

'Tree? Can't say I've seen it. Come on, we'll go and look.'

The car door was open. The vicar stared at it. 'Damn it! I locked that . . . someone's been in here.'

Hurriedly, he checked his car radio and glove box. 'Nothing gone though. You look for your tree, and I'll go and ask Mrs Hughes . . .' Still talking, he went back up the drive. Alick dived into the car and scrabbled under the seats, then ran his hand down gaps and crannies. Nothing. Nothing but a few golden hairs, strangely stiff and bright. He was wondering about them when the vicar came back.

'She didn't open it. Says there've been people hanging about the place though. Strangers. Still, no harm. Did you find it?'

'No.'

'It may have fallen in the boxes.' The vicar closed the door. 'I've taken them over to Ashton Bailey chapel. You're welcome to look.'

Ashton Bailey. Famous for its tombs. Stone knights, crusaders. Like the picture in Luke's mirror. 'Thanks,' Alick said, starting up the drive. 'I will.'

•

Twenty minutes later he was standing in Luke's house.

'They've moved!'

Luke nodded, both hands leaning on the corners of the table. On the Fidchell board the pieces were scattered, black and gold, in a confused huddle. Some had fallen over. Alick wanted to pick them up, but Luke warned him not to touch them. He was studying their positions carefully.

'I should say,' he murmured, 'that they've got the scent. See how they are gathering together?'

'You talk as if they move themselves.'

'And so they do. Not that you ever see it, however long you look. See what I mean.' He pointed to a golden knight. Alick blinked. A minute ago it had been on the other side of the board.

'So . . . who decides the moves?'

'They do. There are two players,' Luke said, 'but they can only watch. That's their fate. The game cannot be stopped till one side or other gets the tree, or . . .' he put his thin extra finger on the empty square in the centre of the board, '. . . or we put it back here. Then the board will be balanced.'

'Your tree has gone, too.'

'There is only one tree.'

Alick frowned over that. 'But I saw two. One here and one on the other board.'

Luke shrugged. 'You may have. But there is only one, and that is the one you took. This board,' he waved a hand at it, 'and the other two like it, merely show us what happens. The board in the hill is, if you like, the master board, the real game.'

'So there are two others?'

'Only three left in the world; each guarded.'

'By whom?'

Luke smiled slowly. 'And wouldn't you like to know! By others like me, those that are half of one world and half of another.' He looked closely at Alick. 'You must have guessed?'

Alick shrugged. 'I suppose so. You mean . . .' he struggled for words, 'you're related to Them?'

The conjuror grinned. 'Sort of. We have strange blood in our family. But we must get on.' He went to a drawer in the dresser and pulled out a small round box, like the one the ointment had been in. He threw it to Alick. 'Here. This is only for emergencies. Don't open it unless you absolutely can't do anything else. I'll have this.' He put a thin wand of peeled hazel in his pocket. 'I've been working on it all night. It will have the power to scatter Them over the board, and they'll take time to regroup. It may help.'

Alick pocketed the box and watched the conjuror wind a scarf round his neck. Then he said, 'I've been to the vicar's. The tree isn't there, but I found these.'

Luke took the hairs and held them up to the light. 'Well. This means they're ahead of us.'

'It's at Ashton Bailey, isn't it?'

Luke nodded. 'Now don't say too much when we get outside. The wood is full of movement; we're bound to be watched.'

Rather unhappily, Alick followed him out into the snow, the slam of the door echoing ominously in his ears. They took a short cut through a thick larch plantation that would bring them out on to the main road beyond the village. It took only ten minutes steady walking for Alick to feel uneasy. He glanced around.

'Oh, they're here all right,' Luke muttered. 'Since we left the house.'

Alick couldn't see anything, but he believed it. They began to hurry. The going was wet and difficult, the path sometimes clear and sometimes blocked by drifts as high as Alick's knees. And it got dark. The darkness closed in — it seemed to ooze out of the trees, so thick that it seemed Luke was forcing his way through a black, solid resistance. The branches creaked and swished, invisible above their heads.

The feeling of oppression, of hidden watchers, was getting on Alick's nerves. 'How far to the Cross?'

'About ten minutes.' Luke sounded worried. 'I didn't think they'd start so soon. Keep close, and don't look behind you. *Don't!* Understand?'

He nodded. But from the corners of his eyes he could already see the shadows moving with them, just out of sight, like reflections that move and flicker in a grimy mirror. And then he began to feel it — the soft touching on his shoulders, a light tapping, something brushing his hair, soft and cold and clinking. He was shivering and couldn't stop.

'Luke . . .'

The conjuror stopped, clenched his fists, then turned around. He looked straight over Alick's shoulder, staring at whatever was there, calmly. At once Alick felt the coldness loosen from his neck. Something backed away.

'Further,' Luke said.

A rustle.

'Get in front of me, Alick,' Luke said quietly, and he obeyed, keeping his eyes firmly ahead.

It was an incredible relief to have Luke behind him, but as they went on, the snow splashed in his face, and he didn't know the path. Luke muttered instructions, but Alick kept his eyes ahead. Finally, the trees ended. They stepped out on to the road at Halcombe Cross.

48

Gaunt, misshapen, the finger of stone marked the heart of the wood. It was old, it had been a trysting-place, a market, a gallows, but the original purpose was long forgotten. Strange marks and carvings adorned it; a rough cross, and under that, pagan rings and spirals and letters from forgotten alphabets.

Alick leaned on it, breathing hard.

'Don't stop,' Luke warned.

The roads were deserted, already thick with snow. On the modern fingerpost a bird was perched, black and silent.

'Come on!' Grabbing his elbow the conjuror strode with him roughly down the road towards Ashton. Alick gasped for breath, but Luke would not slow down, and he constantly glanced over his shoulder.

And then Alick knew why. The certainty came in the silence and tension of the forest. A great host was moving after them down the white road; a crowd of shapes, creaking, and rustling and padding. Their shadows, long and black, stretched out before him. Fingers touched him again, icy coldness closing at his neck.

Suddenly, Luke shoved him ahead and whirled round on his enemies. Surprised, Alick stumbled and fell his length in the wet snow, and at once the road was aflame with an astounding brilliance and a rumbling and roaring that rang in the trees around him. He jerked his head.

Two huge white eyes roared through a torn mist. Luke stood before them, his figure small and dark, half lost in the eerie swirling smoke and the dark bulk screeching down on him.

Then the lorry swerved. With a scream of brakes it careered past them down the road and slithered to a stop.

The cab door was flung open and a head poked out. '*What* the 'ell do you think you're doing, mate?'

Luke grabbed Alick's arm and hauled him towards the lorry. Mist snaked after them.

'You drunk or something?' the driver asked, seeing them loom up in the dimness.

'No. Listen, can you give us a lift along the road? To Ashton?'

The man laughed. 'It's barely five minutes walk!'

'I know. Will you?'

'Oh, all right. Get in round the other side.'

As he climbed up the step, Alick glanced back. Something misty hung there, hardly visible. In the cab the radio was playing loudly. The driver whistled the tune cheerfully through his teeth. With a great hiss and shudder the lorry started. He changed gear noisily.

'Could've been killed, in the road like that!' he yelled above the music. 'Snow, patchy fog. Dangerous!'

Luke nodded. His face was pale; his fingers deep in pockets.

The lorry dropped them half a mile further on. When it had roared away, Alick looked at the conjuror.

'Are you all right?'

'Quite.' Luke climbed the fence. 'But we'll have to take more care. I can see how they're moving. With me out of the way, you'd be on your own, and easy prey for them.'

Alick didn't like the thought of that at all.

8

Ashton Bailey

Along the road ran a metal fence, old-fashioned and bent. Luke jumped over and began to push through the undergrowth. Alick followed, getting snow flicked all over him from the springy branches. Soon they stepped out on to a track, very straight, running into dimness. The trees above were thick and black, and withered grass poked up between frozen puddles.

'Gloomy,' Alick muttered.

Luke crossed the track and tugged ivy from what seemed to be a rock. Half smothered in the leaves was a standing stone.

'There's another,' Alick pointed ahead. 'And one over there. It's an avenue.'

'It is. This will help them; it's their sort of place.'

The weight of oppression, of being watched, had lifted from Alick. He felt careless of danger.

'Feng shui,' he said suddenly.

Luke laughed. 'Yes. A lot of good trying to tell you that, though. You and your sceptical friend!'

'Oh, Jamie's all right.' He stopped, struck by a thought. 'You made his leg worse, didn't you? On purpose!'

Luke had the grace to look confused. 'Well, a bit. Not much, though. I wanted him out of the way. Stupid of me, but I thought he might be the one to go poking his nose into things. How wrong can you get.'

Alick thought about that for a while. Then he said, 'I've always thought . . . the wood has more in it, than you can see. It's a special place.'

'It's Their place, Alick. The wood is a web of danger. We're just trespassers.'

'Like that man who drowned?'

Luke sighed, and was silent. Ice splintered under their feet. Then he said, 'I was too late that day.'

As they walked on, it grew darker. Waxy laurels sprouted on each side, their berries black and poisonous. The ditch stank of fungi and stagnation. Alick pulled the scarf over his nose in disgust, and then noticed the small square tower ahead.

'There's one thing in our favour,' Luke said, blowing on his cold fingers. 'The church.'

The gate clanged noisily behind them. Alick followed the conjuror up the path and stood close behind as Luke turned the great round handle. The door rumbled, and swung slowly open.

The chapel was quiet and empty. Bunches of fresh holly and mistletoe were piled in the middle of the floor, and next to them three large boxes that Alick recognized from the vicar's car. There were no benches; the church was derelict, and only used for the candlelight carol service on Christmas

Eve — a tradition that went back to medieval times. It was bitterly cold. The famous tombs, with their figures of knights and ladies, lay under a coating of frost.

Luke went in, snow swirling behind him. 'Come on.'

He tipped the contents of the first box out, and began sifting through them. Echoes ran around the walls. Alick opened the next. Candles, hymn-books, hassocks and papers, jammed together, damp to the touch. It was as he tugged a sheaf of papers out that he heard it, the tiny, melodious tinkle.

'It's here!' He groped about at the bottom. Then, with a laugh that rang in the roof, grasped the edge of a stone tomb and hauled himself to his feet, the gold and black tree glittering in his hand.

Luke sat back on his heels. He looked relieved.

Then Alick gasped, jerked his head. The stone hand of the knight on the tomb had closed around his wrist.

'Luke!'

'Be quiet!' The conjuror was already there. The knight lay on its slab, eyes closed. It was stone. Its hands were stone. This was impossible.

'It's holding me! I can't get out!'

'Quiet!' Feverishly the conjuror searched his pockets. Then suddenly he turned around.

'What's the matter?'

Luke ignored him. 'Show yourselves!' he said to the empty chapel. Nothing seemed different. But now there was a shadow outside the windows; a mass of shadows.

Luke took a step forward. He had the hazel wand in his hand. 'There's been a mistake,' he said quietly. 'You should go back. The game is over.'

'The game is just begun.'

53

Alick jumped. The whisper had come echoing round the walls.

'No.' Luke's eyes travelled round the room, as if he saw things Alick could not.

'Friend, it begins here.'

A rustle in the corner. Alick twisted, shouted, the door slammed open. In a whirlwind of dust and leaves, a cascade of black and gold shapes arched over them, hung, crashed down.

'Luke!' Alick squirmed in the stone grip. Stones and leaves fell on him, stuck to his hands and face, knocked him to his knees. Arms over head he clung to the effigy, hand-cuffed in stone, under the uproar of wind and dust. Luke reeled backwards — was slammed to the floor — but as he fell he raised the wand and swept it before him. Vivid white sparks stung Alick's eyes.

It ended as quickly as it had begun.

When he was ready, Alick uncovered his face. Dust and dead leaves coated the floor, and rose in clouds from his clothes. Luke was lying by an overturned box.

'Luke!'

The conjuror was still, crooked. Alick knew he would not answer. Fiercely he tugged at the stone hand. 'Let me go, damn it!' The tree was in his pocket. What if they came back for it now? But no. He had time.

Then he saw the white rod. Luke must have dropped it — it lay on the floor nearby. However he stretched, his hand couldn't reach it . . . but perhaps with his foot?

He pushed himself as far out from the tomb as he could, stretched towards the stick. Inch by inch his foot strained for it; cramps attacked his toes, the stone grip seared his skin. Another inch — and he touched. Would it roll away?

54

Painfully, he rolled the wand, dragged it, scooped it in, until it was close enough to pick up.

A peeled hazel stick, white and thin. Now he had got it, he didn't know what to do with it. How did it work? He touched the stone glove with one end. Nothing happened. Tugging was no use; his wrist was sore and bleeding from that. A stone. Get a stone and smash it. Putting the stick in his trapped hand he bent down to fumble for a broken tile — and fell over! It had let him go! Or rather, he thought, rubbing his aching wrist, he had gone through it as if it was sand.

He turned to Luke. The conjuror's eyes were closed, his forehead lay on the stone floor. He was cold, and shaking his shoulder had no result. Alick bit his lip. His fingers felt the conjuror's pulse. He didn't even know if it was fast or slow. That first aid class, he thought. Sat at the back and talked. What a fool.

He would have to go for help. Cautiously, he went to the door. Outside it was snowing again. The wood was a web of white driven flakes. He was on his own. They'd got what They wanted.

Alick went back. 'Please, Luke! Wake up!' No use. He didn't seem hurt, perhaps it was some sort of spell. Finally, Alick found a pencil and a scrap of paper, wrote 'Gone for help' and pushed it under the conjuror's cold fingers.

When he turned, the white dog was sitting in the doorway. It padded softly past him and sat down, then looked at him.

'Tell him I've gone on,' Alick said suddenly. The dog lay down, chin on paws. He felt stupid, and yet . . . 'I'll take care of the tree. Look after Luke.' Then he marched out into the snow, pulling the door behind him. After about ten steps, he remembered that the hazel twig was still in his pocket.

Should he leave it? No. After all, They were probably still about.

Plunging hands in pockets, he began to plough up the long avenue. Gloom seeped into him with the cold and the wet. What a mess. Where was he to go? What should he do? Ahead, the standing stones began, a tall one loomed at the side of the track and a shorter one leaned opposite it. Among the flung blurs of snow, their edges seemed like faces, hook-nosed, gaunt. After a moment's consideration, Alick stepped off the track and plunged into the wood.

9

The Oak Tree

He had once been a Boy Scout for two years — he knew all about compasses and guiding yourself by the stars and blazing your trail. Despite that, in ten minutes he was totally lost. Everything was black and white, straight trees and flying snow; the sky, when he glimpsed it, a horrible dead yellow. The blizzard was almost horizontal, blinding him, soaking the front of his clothes and numbing his face and hands. He had tried to cut marks in the trees with his latchkey, but it was useless. Stumbling, he struggled on. If he kept this way he was sure to get back to the road, sure to.

The snow lay in humps and hollows; often he sank knee-deep in drifts. Blackthorn and bramble spread nets to tangle him. At one point the snow suddenly collapsed. He found himself gasping ankle-deep in an ice cold stream, and as he jerked his hands out of his pockets to balance himself, the white stick fell out and into the water. Wordless, he watched it float swiftly away.

On the bank he wrung out his socks, stamped about to get his feet warm, and put the tree in his shirt pocket inside his pullover. As he moved it, the tiny leaves tinkled, and he closed his hand over it quickly. For a second he had sensed the wood listening. The sudden silence was enormous. All around him, nothing for miles and miles but the trees, their humps and hollows, their boughs and boles and branches. He was all alone in it, and small.

It was then he heard the bang. Not very far ahead. Familiar. Normal. It took him a second to pin it down. A car door, slamming. After a second's astonishment he shouldered through the snowy bushes to his right and almost fell out on to a narrow gravel track. There in front of him, solid stone and with a warm comfortable light in its windows, was the last thing he had ever expected to see — a pub.

Where on earth was he?

Puzzled, he limped through the car park and stopped under the sign.

It creaked and swung under its coating of ice. The Oak Tree. He really must be lost. Still, he thought thankfully, they're bound to have a telephone or something.

He made his way round to the front and peered in through the window, rubbing snow from the glass. There were only about nine or ten people inside, most at the bar or sitting down, two playing darts. Boldly, he pushed the door open and went in.

The smell of beer and cigarettes struck him, and the drowsy, airless warmth of a hot room. Heads turned. He felt suddenly small, and wet and scruffy.

'Well! What happened to you!' The barmaid laughed and put down her cloth.

Alick felt the snow slide off his boots. 'I'm sorry,' he muttered.

'*And* you're under age.' She winked at a man at the bar.

'I haven't come in for a drink.'

The customers chortled. 'Don't mind her, son,' one of them said. 'She's just kidding you.'

Alick smiled, uncomfortably. He went up to the bar, hoping they'd stop staring at him and carry on their talk.

'How far am I from Halcombe?' he asked quietly.

'About four miles.'

He groaned, silently. 'Have you got a phone?'

'I'm sorry, my love,' the barmaid said. 'It's out of order. Snow, I expect. We're waiting for the engineer.'

He might have known. Nothing was going right — perhaps 'They' had even pulled the lines down. He had hoped to get help for Luke, but now he saw he was on his own.

He must have looked as dejected as he felt.

'Come over and sit by the fire, love,' the girl was saying. 'You're wet through. Take your coat off and have a nice hot cup of tea.'

He shouldn't stop; he ought not to waste time. And yet . . . After a second's hesitation, he pulled off his gloves and undid the wet thongs of his duffel coat. He needn't stay long; just to get warm.

He gave her the coat and wandered across the room to the fire. There was a comfortable armchair next to it, but he did not sit down. Better not get too cosy. As he warmed his face and hands, he thought hard. Luke had said the tree had to go back on the board — presumably that meant to Tolbury Tump. He must be six miles or more from there. In the snow and growing darkness, it would take him hours — even if he got to the road it would be choked with snow-drifts by now. Traffic must have all but stopped. Well, at least that meant his father would have to stay in Gloucester . . . if only he didn't phone Jamie's house!

Alick sighed. He would have to walk to the Tump — there was no other way. He was beginning to wish he had stayed with Luke.

The fireplace was wooden, carved with old twisting snakes and stems. Above it, a large mirror reflected the room. He looked up at it. The barmaid was hanging up his coat on a peg by the door. And as he watched he was sure he saw her hand slip out of his pocket. She hung the coat up, and went into the kitchen.

Despite the fire, he felt cold. The tree, small and hard, was in his shirt pocket; he could feel it against his chest. Was that what she was looking for?

Some of the customers were looking at him; two men at the bar. They had hard, black eyes, and high, hooked noses; somehow familiar. They leaned easily on the bar, but did not drink. They pretended to talk, but their eyes were on him. The hairs on the back of his hands bristled with tension. He knew now. "They" were here! He wasn't certain how many, but they were here all right; watching.

A few more men came in, laughing, and went to the bar. Some dogs slipped in behind them. If the roads were blocked, how did they all get out here? Sixteen, seventeen now. Was it all of them? The fire crackled cheerfully. Steam rose from his damp knees.

'Now then, how about some tea?'

The barmaid was at his elbow, with a tray. On it was a large mug of steaming liquid and a plate of cakes — small sponge cakes with buttery icing.

'How much will it cost?'

'Oh, never mind that,' she said. 'Go and sit down . . . sit in

that armchair there by the fire.' She nodded at the big chair with its soft, enticing cushions. He sighed, thought, Why not? and was about to step towards it when he glanced in the mirror.

Every eye in the room was on him.

The drinkers were not drinking, talk had died, the dart players had forgotten their game. Even the landlord was leaning on the bar, studying him.

'Go on,' said the girl, impatiently. 'What's the matter?'

He looked at her. Her eyes were black, bird-like. Something bright sparkled in her hair.

'Sit down!' she commanded.

Suddenly, overwhelmingly, fear washed over him. He could not move — No! Keep still, think! Knight, minstrel, king, lady and bird; they were all here. From the corner of his eye he saw the carved serpents on the fireplace rustle. He did the only thing he could think of; plunged his hand in his pocket and brought out the conjuror's box.

At once the girl dropped her tray and grabbed at him with a scream. The men at the bar leapt from their stools and flung themselves forward. But the lid was off.

It was dark, and cold. Snow settled slowly on his pullover. He was standing six inches from the edge of a sheer cliff. It plummeted down into the forest, bushes springing out from its side. As he stood there, a rock slipped and bounced, crashing down endlessly into emptiness. One more step, that's all it would have needed. One more step . . .

Ten minutes later he realized he was sitting on a stone in the snow, staring stupidly at nothing. Shock. He had to pull

61

himself together. Getting up, he stamped about, shivering. The box was still in his hand. It was empty, but the inside was coated with black powder, like soot. He touched it gently, then realized that the stuff was all over his hands and clothes, and was blowing about in the wind. Black smudges darkened the snow.

He put the lid back on and put it in his pocket, then washed his face and hands with snow, rubbing vigorously until his skin tingled. His coat and scarf hung on a bush. He pulled them on and gazed around.

It was a small clearing in the wood, that was all. Where the door had been was a crushed trail of nettles. The whole thing, pub, fire, chair, had been an illusion, made for him. One more step and he would be lying down there now, badly injured if not worse, and those Things pawing him for the tree. No wonder Luke had been worried.

He began to march in what he hoped was the right direction. Things were bad — he must hurry. They knew where he was, but he was hopelessly lost, and had used up Luke's box. He was also cold, tired, and hungry — the memory of those cakes was a torment. And it was almost dark. He *had* to find the road.

An hour later, leaning on a tree-trunk to catch his breath, he knew he could not do it. The wood, they said, had twenty million trees, and he was blundering further and further into the middle of it. Down here among the aisles of trunks, the snow lay in drifts; dark branches overhead hid the stars. And the silence was the worst — the unbroken winter stillness. As he moved on, even his footsteps were muffled. The snow stopped, then began to freeze slowly on the ground. He was walking into trees now, and bushes, it was so dark, and the tiny threads of path led him nowhere. Worst of all, he began to imagine he was walking in circles; was sure he recognized trees he had passed ten minutes ago. Trees, trees, trees.

Until he saw the light.

Yes! There it was! Ahead of him, a little way off to the left. A warm, red light, flickering.

But Alick was wary. Once bitten . . . he thought, and stood still in the silence, watching it. When he moved at last, it was as slowly and quietly as he could, slipping from tree to tree without a rustle in the wet undergrowth. Soon he was close enough to see.

It was a fire. From behind a thick holly bush he took a good look. The fire lit a small clearing. In the centre of the clearing was an ancient oak stump, rotten and hollow, with a great gash down its side. For five minutes he watched the flames burn and nothing stirred — finally he crept out and warmed his hands. It might be a tramp's fire. A tramp would be a relief.

Then he noticed the tracks, trampled in the snow around the oak stump. A dog's? Or a fox? He got down on hands and knees and looked closer. The crack in the tree was wide. He slipped his head in and waited to get used to the blackness. He saw the outline of a heap of straw, a huddle of what looked like fur. And then the voice spoke, close by his ear in the darkness.

'I've been waiting for you, Alick Webster,' it said.

10

Tod-lowery

Alick froze.

The bundle of furs twitched, stretched out a long thin arm, and grabbed the end of his scarf as it dangled on the floor.

'Come in, sonny. I don't bite — much.'

Tugged suddenly forward, he fell on his hands and knees into the hollow tree, and the bright light of the fire flooded in behind him. It showed a thin weaselly face, straggly hair, rusty whiskers. The creature hugged its knees with bony arms, and the fingers that held his scarf had sharp nails and were covered with short, reddish hair.

'Got the tree?' it asked casually, turning its head sideways and laying it on its knees.

Alick nodded, speechless.

The creature grinned, showing sharp white teeth. 'Good.'

There was nothing else to do. Alick crawled in and leaned

back against the damp bark. The tree was dingy and smelt of wet fur and leaves.

'Tod-lowery,' the thing said, with a wink of one eye. 'That's what you call me. Chicken?'

'What?'

'Chicken. From a farm over Minsterworth way. A bit stringy, but chewable.'

Bewildered, Alick watched the creature fish something out from a corner. It was a chicken leg, badly singed.

'I don't usually bother myself, but I thought you might not like it raw. Take it then!'

Alick took it, rather unwilling.

'Eat it,' the Tod said slyly. 'It's real enough.'

It was. And delicious, since he hadn't eaten for what seemed hours — *was* hours, by now. As he chewed, he watched the creature and the creature watched him.

Finally, he tossed the bone outside and licked his fingers.

'Thanks.'

'And now, a drink.'

It was a murky-looking liquid, in a carved wooden cup. Dubious, he sipped and felt the warmth spread through his chest. As he downed the rest he tried to remember where he had tasted it before, and as he put the cup down it came to him. At Talley. It was the same stuff.

'Now,' the Tod said, 'we can speak. Tell me how you got it.'

'Got what?'

It smiled. 'The Fidchell tree, my innocent.'

The narrow eyes shone in the firelight. Whoever it was, it knew too much already. To his surprise Alick found himself unafraid. He explained how he had gone into Tolbury Tump.

65

The Tod nodded wisely. 'And on that day of all days. So you're the one who started it — the Fidchell.'

'You know about that?'

'Everybody does. It happens.' Seeing Alick was uneasy, it grinned, and wrapped long bony arms around its knees. 'But not for a long time now. *What* a naughty boy we've been. No wonder there's all this fuss.'

'Fuss?'

'Out there.' It nodded towards the opening. 'The wood is alive with them; swarming, like a tipped-up hive. I've heard there's been no end of trouble already.'

'It's not fair!' Alick said suddenly.

The Tod looked surprised. 'That's the game, sonny. Gold and black, sunshine and shadow. They have to be in balance.'

'And who are the players?'

The weaselly face turned sideways. 'So you don't know that either. We are innocent, aren't we? Well then, long ago, little cub, two kings played Fidchell. They played it in an iron-grey fortress, while outside their two armies tore each other to pieces. It was a battle they could have stopped, but neither of them would lose the game.'

Alick stared. 'So what happened?'

'It's said that their punishment for causing all those deaths is that they must play Fidchell until Doomsday, and only on one night in a hundred can they leave the board. Which, I suppose, is where you came in!'

'So they move the pieces?'

'Oh no. Nothing's that simple.' The Tod winked slyly. 'The Fidchell armies play their own game; the players must sit, and watch, and suffer, and not a finger can they raise to help — whatever happens.' He hugged himself gleefully. 'They'll be in a fine state watching this.'

'So am I,' Alick thought. 'What about you?' he asked aloud. 'Aren't you in it?'

'Ah, well, I'm just me. I keep out of it, no one bothers me.' He licked his sharp white teeth. 'Just as well.'

A gust of wind crackled the flames. The Tod's nose wrinkled. 'You smell of wizardry,' it said slowly.

Alick remembered the box. 'I can't smell anything.'

'But I can. What is it?'

He took the box out of his pocket, but kept hold of it.

'And who gave you that?'

'A conjuror.'

The Tod-lowery narrowed its eyes. 'Ah! That'll be the sorcerer at Talley.'

'I thought you might know Luke!'

'I know him.' The Tod grinned. 'And he knows me.'

Perhaps it wasn't such good news. Still, Alick explained about the attack in the ruined chapel.

'Oh, he'll not be hurt, not that one. He'll be about by now.'

'Can you help me to find him? Or to get to Tolbury? I'll never get through by myself.'

'Well now,' the creature scratched idly, 'I might.'

Suddenly Alick wondered if it could be trusted. After that business at the pub he should be much more wary. He put the box away.

'Forget it. I'll go myself.'

'The last one who tried that,' the Tod said casually, 'didn't get far. I found him hanging on a tree, not ten paces from where I left him. Not a pretty sight. Bloody as a dead fox.'

It pulled a flea out of one ear and cracked it.

Alick fidgeted. Then he said, 'Can we start now?'

'No,' the Tod shook its head. 'We'll wait for the moon.

67

They're more than a handful in the dark. You go to sleep now over there. I'll call you.'

Its white teeth glittered. After a moment, Alick shuffled down into the straw. He felt tired, but didn't want to sleep; he wanted to get it all over. But the Tod was in no hurry. It lay down again, yawning and scratching and fidgeting itself, into a comfortable hollow. 'Can I ask you something?' Alick said after a long while.

'Surely.'

'Well, all the time we've been here, you haven't put a bit of wood on that fire, and it's as bright as ever. There's no smoke, either. And how did you know my name?'

But the Tod turned over, and began to snore.

Alick sighed. He hadn't really expected an answer. Through the crack in the tree he could see the snow, falling softly again, smoothing out his footprints. He had lost all count of time; it must be late, after midnight. Where was Luke by now? Was he out there in the wood, or in Halcombe, banging on the bookshop door? Or was he still lying in the cold chapel? Wondering, Alick fell asleep.

When he woke, the Tod-lowery was gone and the fire was out. A wand of moonlight came down through the branches. He sat up, stiff with cold, and felt anxiously for the tree. It was still there, chiming faintly under his fingers. Outside, something howled, long and melancholy. A fox, he thought. After a while it stopped. Then, in the silence, he heard paddings and rustlings in the wood.

He crouched, warily, watching the crack of darkness. Now he could distinguish the sound of hooves; a low thudding in the leaves, that grew louder and closer. The clinking of harnesses began to fill the clearing. Silent, his hands and knees deep in the straw, he watched them pass the crack in the tree; the pale hooves of the horses gleaming in a strange light, the paws of dogs padding past. Someone was playing a harp. The soft notes tugged at him, but he sat still, hardly breathing, every hair and muscle stiff with dread.

It took them at least five minutes to pass — all that silent, jingling troop — and once, to his dismay, a golden dog put its nose to the tree and sniffed, so that the hair prickled on his scalp; but it padded on, and the whole glinting, shimmering army rustled away into silence.

After a few minutes he looked out. The Tod was standing in the glade, a lean shadow. As Alick crawled out he saw the wood was made of black columns rising from a white carpet. And far above the branches, like gems in a net, shone the brilliant frosty stars of December.

'Ready?' The Tod held out a hand — almost a paw, Alick thought — and helped him up. 'Right. That was too close. Now we go my ways, and very odd ways you'll find them. Don't say a word . . . not for anything. If you see anything more of Them, give me a poke in the back, but doubtless I'll have seen them before you. Remember, not a whisper!'

'But where are we going?'

The Tod glared. 'That's a daft remark. Tolbury, where else?'

'Luke might need help.'

'*You* need help!' The Tod grinned. 'Luke can look after himself. He's had plenty of practice. Come on.'

It was a journey Alick never forgot. They walked for hours, under great plantations of trees, in a black and white world. The Tod loped ahead, squeezing through gaps in bushes and under sharp, overhanging rocks, climbing over scree or following invisible threads of paths through the hummocky snow. Often they crossed small streams that had frozen into ice; underfoot the glassy slabs splintered; and bubbles of trapped air slid and creaked.

Many things paused to watch them go by. Badgers, snuffling in the undergrowth; a startled deer; a white owl that twisted its head silently as they passed. The Tod winked at it and it flew off, hoo-hooing gently. And there was a woman, dressed in green who came up to them suddenly out of the trees and spoke a few low words to the Tod. As she passed beside him, Alick shivered at the iciness and the cold sweet smell that hung about her. But he was careful not to ask any questions. When they went on again the Tod grinned at him strangely, eyes and teeth a-glitter in the moonlight.

After that things grew confused. Alick lost himself; walked in a dream or a spell, vaguely aware of wading chest-high through snow (or was it leaves?), of entering tunnels and moving through holes — dark narrow holes littered with branches and rubble and insects that were too large. Size and shape seemed to change; sometimes he was sure the trees were miles above him, bushes were like forests about him, or that he was bent over, long and lean and running on hands and feet. Glimpses of his own hands showed them strange, unfamiliar. Once, at the end of a long ride of oak trees, he saw a dark bird flap ahead of them; its feathers brushed a scatter of snow from the branches. He tapped the Tod and pointed, but the Tod just laughed and shook its head.

Finally, they came to the end of the trees. With a rush, recognition came back to him, and he straightened, easing a strange ache in his back. He knew now where they were. Before him the moonlit fields dipped to the railway line where it ran deep in its cutting into the great tunnel under Corsham Chase. Beyond that, somewhere in the wood, was the Greenmere, and the bald dome of Tolbury Tump.

'Right,' said the Tod. 'You can talk now. We have to cross the field and the silver lines, and this is the hard part, for I have no power once out of the trees. They'll see us for sure.' The foxy face grinned at him. 'Good runner?'

'Sort of. Not very fast though.'

'Isn't that a pity. Well, take a deep breath, and do your best . . .'

'Wait!' Alick said. 'Before we start, was that one of Them, in the wood?'

'No.' Alert, the Tod rubbed its long nose. 'That was just folk, moving. Things are restless. Everyone knows the Fidchell is on. The Ellyll told me.'

'Who?'

'The Ellyll, the icy lady. She said the wood is sealed tight. Nothing can get in or out. And she's heard the sorcerer is looking for you.'

Alick's eyes widened. 'Luke!'

'Ay. I told you, didn't I? He'll be making for the Tump. Now, are you ready?'

'Yes.'

'Let's go!'

They leapt into the white field, floundering rather than running; snow to the knees. But only half-way across, and they heard the whirr of wings above them. Something blotted out the stars.

'Hurry!' the Tod yelled. Ahead, the field was sliced clean. Alick shouldered through the bushes and saw, below him, the railway lines — two tracks of silver in the moonlight. Shadows wheeled over him. He plunged over the side and

71

slithered and scrambled after the Tod, through the stinging nettles and brambles, hitting the bottom cut and sore. The Tod loped over the rails. 'Come on,' it hissed, 'or . . .'

Then it stopped, teeth bared.

'What's wrong?'

The Tod's tongue flickered, tasting the air. 'We're too late, sonny.'

Ahead, the silver lines ran into the tunnel, a great mouth opening in the hillside, its dark entrance dripping with brambles and ferns. Inside it, was blackness; a crowded, clinking, restless, fluttering blackness.

11

Icicles

They were there all right. Horsemen — indistinct in the shadows, but the glitter of their weapons was unmistakable, all colour toned down to a ghostly grey. Pennants and banners floated above them. Shields were slung on arm or saddle-bow. And behind, deeper in the tunnel, other shapes lurked, long and sinuous.

In all the trees of the cutting the ravens came down, silently — a black snow.

'What now?' Alick muttered.

'Not much. You'll have to give it up.'

'I won't!'

The Tod grinned, its eyes on the tunnel. 'That's my boy. We'll doubtless think of something.'

A horseman was moving forward, harness clinking. Slowly his horse came on over the snow, leaving no prints, having no shadow. The rider was helmeted, only his eyes visible. Alick waited, fists clenched. He hadn't come all this

73

way for nothing. He wouldn't give it up. Think of something!

The shining beast stopped. The knight gently dropped the point of his spear an inch from Alick's face, and left it there. The wicked steel menaced his eyes. Still he did not move.

'He wants that tree,' the Tod muttered, unnecessarily.

'He can whistle for it.'

The spear fell, its point touched his chest. Then, eyes impassive, the knight pushed. Alick felt the point push through his clothes, then shove, painfully, against his breastbone.

He stepped back. 'All right. Have the damn thing.'

Slowly, his hand went to his coat buttons. As he took out the tree, dragging each second out as long as he could, the tiny leaves tinkled in the wind, glittering gold and black.

And then, with a bounce and a flutter a raven came from nowhere and landed on the spear, weighing it suddenly down. The horse moved back, uneasy; the knight whipped up his weapon angrily.

It was then Alick had his idea. Both sides, ravens and knights, wanted the tree. To get it was to win. While he had it both sides were against him, united, but if he gave it to one side, the other would fight them for it. Divide and conquer.

Suddenly, he held the tree high, so the moonlight caught it. Every eye swivelled to it, a small, glinting, mystical object. Then he flung it, hard and fast, into the tunnel — or pretended to. Every head turned, seeking the small thing in the blackness of the sky. Alick shoved it back quickly into his pocket. but as he stared he saw to his amazement the flash and glitter of it falling from the stars high over the horsemen into the tunnel's mouth. But he hadn't thrown it!

Chaos erupted. The knight wheeled and rode. Birds and riders poured into the tunnel; shriek and howl and sword-slash rang in the cutting. For a moment he and the Tod were forgotten. And then, as they watched the black semi-circle in the hill, the change began.

Icicles grew suddenly, swiftly, without sound. Down like a portcullis they fell, like a frozen curtain, spreading and joining and spilling, hard as rock, on to the snow. Sealed with seamed glass, the tunnel's mouth was white and hard.

'Alick,' said a voice. 'Up here.'

High on the embankment, Luke was watching them, hands in pockets. Behind him a white horse nuzzled the snow.

Shoved from behind by the Tod, who was snorting and chortling with glee, Alick scrambled to the top. The horse raised his head and watched him with narrow red eyes.

Luke caught the bridle. 'Can you ride?'

'Not much.'

'It doesn't matter.' Luke swung himself up. 'Just get behind me, Tam Lin will manage us.'

'Put your feet here.' The Tod crouched and clasped its hands. Alick put his foot in, but did not jump.

'Hurry up!' the bent figure snapped.

'Luke. I didn't throw it . . .'

The Tod snorted.

'I know.' Luke was watching the tunnel. 'But you saw it.'

'He means he conjured it up,' the Tod snapped. 'Now, are you getting on this creature or not?'

Alick scrambled up. Once it felt him there, the horse turned its head and paced into the wood. The moon stroked them with brief silver fingers.

'That trick with the icicles,' the Tod declared, 'that was the best ever, laddie.'

Luke nodded, serious. 'It was risky. It could have brought the whole thing down on top of you.'

He sounded tired, Alick thought. He held the conjuror's coat with both hands.

'I didn't know you had a horse.'

'There are a lot of things you don't know,' Luke observed.

'And you've met this horse before, though he might have looked different.'

Alick thought of the face in the shaving-mirror.

'I was glad to see you,' he said. 'I was worried stiff in that church.'

The conjuror shook his head. 'You did all right,' he said. 'Tam Lin was waiting for me, that was maybe an hour after you'd gone. I found your note.' He slapped the horse's neck affectionately. 'I was sore and cold and worried. There was terror running in the wood. Trees were down on every road. You'd been seen running, and in a glamour.'

'A what?'

'A sort of spell. I don't know what they tried, but when I got there I knew you were all right, because of the box. Then someone said you were with the Tod. I stopped worrying after that.'

The Tod, loping at the horse's side, laughed, and bowed with a flourish.

'We tracked you from the lair,' Luke said. 'It wasn't easy.' He and the Tod exchanged a knowing look. 'Now, hang on. We haven't got time to waste.'

As the horse ran, the wood loomed like a black wall in front of them. Before Alick could gasp, they arrowed down a path like a crack in masonry. Clutching Luke's coat he twisted and glanced back, saw far behind them a long red form loping. The fox sped after them, bending its sly, whiskered face sometimes to lick the cool snow. Alick clung on, out of the wind, thinking of his living-room over the shop, with its snug fire and the Christmas tree loaded with tinsel and coloured globes. And his father's present — a pullover and two books and a tin of tobacco — all wrapped up in the bottom of his wardrobe. If I don't get back, he thought, how will he know where they are?

'Alick!' Luke yelled irritably. 'Hold on! You're falling asleep!'

With a jerk he gripped tight, and opened his eyes. The horse slowed and stopped. Alick slipped off, thankfully, and stamped about, banging his arms against his body and rubbing the agonizing chill out of his ears. 'Sorry. I couldn't help it.'

The Tod-lowery ambled out of the trees, grinning, and Luke took it aside, talking quietly. It nodded, waved at Alick, and was gone.

'Drink this,' Luke said, crossing to him. 'It'll wake you up.'

Alick took a swig. Hot, searing liquid struck the back of his throat like a flame-thrower. Gasping, he handed it back. 'Did you make that?' he managed.

Luke laughed. 'I wish I could! It's brandy.' He took a drink and screwed the top on, his hands clumsy with cold. 'Come on. The last lap.'

The next half-hour was the worst. Despite the bitter cold, Alick found it hard to keep awake, and when he did his hunger was painful. That chicken leg must have been hours ago. And not only that — as they came nearer the Greenmere he began to feel that terror that Luke had talked about. Owls flapped about them as they rode; the trees were full of creaking wind; small animals scattered and screeched as they thundered by. On the last part of the path Luke slowed the horse. Progress was difficult. Branches had been torn down and scattered; the spilt and trampled berries were black as blood. As they went on it was harder; whole saplings had been uprooted, and finally a great bank of snow, as high as the horse's head, reared before them. They had to stop.

Luke sat there, silent for a second. Then he whistled, low and clear. The answer came from far off towards Tolbury; the eerie bark of a fox. Luke turned the horse's head. 'The wood is sealed,' he said grimly. 'So we'll have to go another way, one they might not expect.'

The horse whinnied and blew through its nostrils, then it turned off the path and pushed through some bushes.

'Hang on now, Alick,' Luke said in his firmest voice.

They came out of the trees. There lay the Greenmere, its surface shining strangely. Daintily, the horse stepped down to it, crushing the pine needles and the frosty white stalks of grass. Its forehooves clattered on the Mere. It stepped out, and the polished surface was as smooth and firm as a marble floor. The Greenmere was frozen.

Astounded, Alick gazed down. A perfect reflection of his face stared back at him. The mirror-horse below licked the tongue of its replica.

'Will it hold our weight?'

'I don't know,' Luke said. 'Anyway, we've no choice.'

'And if it breaks?'

'Don't ask.'

12

Sealed

Luke nudged the horse on with his knees. Blowing and tossing its head, it gave him an unreadable look and began to walk. The silver hooves rang on the glassy surface, and strange, wheezing sounds came from the ice, as if it would crack and splinter underneath them. Breath held, Alick waited, expecting any minute the crack, the dark star of water and the sudden toppling. But, despite a few slips, the white horse walked out into the middle of the Mere and stood there, snorting clouds of breath from its nostrils.

'Come on, Tam,' the conjuror murmured. 'Don't listen to them. That's what they want.'

The horse paced, ears pricked. Behind the splintering, Alick could hear it too, a muffled sound, like people shouting to be heard, and banging on some thick door between them and you. Angry, frustrated voices. Then he realized where they were coming from.

Beneath the horse's hooves, beneath the green glass of

the ice, shapes moved. Broad hands splayed against the barrier; a host of faces mouthed muffled threats. Alick heard beaks pecking, swords hammering; he looked away, but Luke had already felt his grip tighten. 'Ease up, Alick,' he said gently. 'You're pinching.'

'Sorry.' Alick stared straight ahead. If they fell . . . If the ice splintered up like a row of green teeth and swallowed them . . . but he told himself not to think about it. It was too late now.

Then, like a pistol shot, the ice cracked. Tam Lin staggered; Alick grabbed Luke tight. The ice heaved, jolted apart, a hand came out of it, then a sword, a body in armour, and at that moment the horse put his forehooves on the first cracked reed on the shore. At once Luke kicked him into speed, and behind them, as they rode, the Greenmere erupted with a roar and crash as if some mighty iceberg was smashing through the surface.

Over the soft wet snow they galloped, out of the trees and on to the floundering whiteness of Tolbury Tump. The sky was dark; a thin moon trailed rags of cloud.

Luke jumped down and Alick leapt after him. They fell into the snowy bushes breathlessly, the cries from the lake roaring through the wood. Luke snatched up a stone and struck it against the rock until it rang among the clamour. But the door did not open.

'Try again!' Alick yelled, but Luke shook his head and flung the stone away. 'It's sealed. I expected it.'

The crack of a twig made them spin.

'Tod?'

The long, grinning face slid round a tree.

'Still here?'

'Oh, I had to see this one through.' Tod bit its nails.

'What are you going to do?' Behind him the ring of the hollow was a mass of shadows. Luke ignored them. 'Where's Tam?'

'Here.'

Alick stared in surprise. Into the hollow jumped a tall slim boy, his white hair glimmering in the moonlight. He wore pale clothes and carried a spear; a gold collar gleamed about his neck.

'They're coming,' he said. 'Gold and black together.'

'Open the door!' Alick shouted. The tree stuck in his chest and he pulled it out and flung it down. 'I've brought the damn thing back! What else am I supposed to do!'

'Quiet!' The conjuror put all twelve fingers together and blew on them. 'All right, I'll do it. Tod, Tam, I'll need time. Just five minutes.'

The Tod grinned, 'My pleasure. This should be good.'

'It will be,' Luke glanced at Alick. 'If it works.'

In seconds they were alone. Two sinuous streaks, one white, one red, flashed over the lip of the hollow. Growls and cries and the screams of horses rang around them. Fox and hound flung themselves on the foremost riders.

'No questions,' Luke ordered, before Alick could open his mouth. He pulled boxes of oddments hastily from his pockets. Horns rang below them; green phosphorescent flashes lit the sky.

'Take your boots off. Socks too.'

'What!'

'Do it!'

Grumbling, Alick obeyed. His feet were blue in the bitter air.

'Sit still!' Falling on his knees the conjuror dipped his finger into a box of ointment, dabbed it on the undersides of

Alick's feet and then on the tops. It was icy, but Alick clamped his teeth shut and endured it. Luke worked hurriedly, humming and muttering to himself. As Alick jerked his socks back on, the backs of his hands were anointed, then his forehead, his neck, the small of his back — all were dabbed with the icy cream. When it was finished, tiny rings of cold lay on the extremes of his body. As he stood, he could feel the cross of ice creep up and join with swift, stabbing pains.

'Here! Don't forget this.' The Fidchell tree was shoved into his hands. 'Put it back where you found it!'

'What!'

'Back where you found it!' Luke yelled, shoving him to the door. Vivid green lights were flickering in the sky; the screech of a fox and the clang of swords rang down the hillside. Alick hung on to the cliffside, transfixed by cold. The strange hands of the conjuror turned him to face the rock, pushed him hard on each spread hand, each foot, on back, on head. He screamed. The rock softened, welcomed him. Its cold grip folded him in blackness. It gripped his hands, his feet; he could not turn his head. Luke was somewhere, shouting, kneeling in the snow behind him, far, far behind. Down a tunnel of blackness he was sucked, absorbed, and the rock took hold of him and tore him fiercely through.

Outside, a spear clanged against the rock.

Luke stood up slowly, and turned to face the dark ring of horsemen around the hollow.

13

The Fortress

Alick was lying in dirt and blackness. A spider ran across the back of his neck, and he shook it off as he sat up. Blood ran from a cut on his face. His body felt as if it did not belong to him, as if it had been frozen and thawed again, or gone through some extremity of pain.

The tunnel, he found, standing up, was just as it had been before, a filthy crack in the hill. But the odd thing was that he could see right through the door. He knew it was there, but as he put his hand up it sank in gently, and it was hard to tug out again.

Outside, he saw that Luke was standing with his back to him, hands clenched. A spear lay on the ground. In the dimness round the hollow clustered a great host of shadows, black and formless. Luke was speaking, but no sound came in to Alick. He saw the Tod lope up, and Tam Lin, behind him, picked up the spear.

But what now? Put the tree back, Luke had said, but still

Alick hesitated. He couldn't leave them out there. Not like this. He shoved the tree into his pocket and fumbled over the door. There must be a way to open it. His fingers stubbed on hardening rock. No knob, no handle.

Already the lip of the hollow was seething with birds, rising and swirling like black smoke from a cauldron. One of them launched itself at Luke. The conjuror ducked, and Tam Lin stabbed the thing with the spear. Black feathers crashed against the rock.

A lock, a lever, anything! His hands groped. He kicked and slammed the rock in fury. Birds were falling like black rain. The Tod bit and snapped, his lithe body twisting in the air. Luke flung his arm over his eyes.

Nothing! And after all, Alick thought suddenly, why should there be? This was no ordinary door. 'Open!' he yelled, hands flat, commanding. 'Open!'

The rock shuddered, swung; noise erupted from outside. It was a battlefield. As the golden light hit them, the birds screamed; their eyes were gilt studs in blackness. A waterfall of horses roared into the hollow.

Luke must have felt the rock move against him; he grabbed the Tod. 'Leave it! Get inside!'

They dived in beside Alick and threw themselves against the door. 'Tam Lin!' the conjuror yelled. Slowly the great rocks moved together; a white body slithered in, behind it a lance head snapped, a bird's wing was crushed. Then the line of light closed up and sealed tight. Feathers and dust settled.

For a while they sat wearily in a breathless row; Luke and the Tod bleeding on face and hands, Tam Lin smiling strangely. Finally Alick rubbed tired eyes with his sleeve.

'They can't get in now, can they?'

His voice echoed down the tunnel. Dimly he saw Luke shrug.

'Not through this door. There are other ways.'

He gazed at Alick. 'I told you to go on. We would have been all right.'

'It didn't look like it!'

'It's not us they want. It's the tree.' The conjuror tossed the Tod a handkerchief, and with a grin the creature dabbed daintily at a cut.

'Sorry.' Alick said bitterly. 'Next time.'

'I'm not ungrateful,' Luke said quickly, 'but we've lost time and that's important. Still, it's probably just as well. This part isn't likely to be easy.' He stood up. 'Come on. I'll lead, then you, Alick. Tam last, if you will.'

As they rose, the Tod clapped Alick's shoulder. 'Whatever he says,' he whispered, 'I'm damned glad to be out of *that*, little cub.'

Alick grinned. Then, hands stretched, he shuffled into the darkness. The passage was as narrow and contorted as before, but soon Alick came to realize that the twists were tighter and more sudden, as if somehow the tunnel had shifted and wriggled in the earth. Ahead, in the dimness, Luke's shadow stumbled as he felt his way; behind, the Tod kept a firm grip on Alick's coat.

Not only did the tunnel twist wrongly, but it began to run steeply downhill. Alick knew they should have reached the Fidchell hall a long time ago.

Then Luke stopped. A cool draught moved against Alick's face. 'Are we there?'

His voice rang double. Luke shook his head. 'The tunnel forks in two.'

'That's impossible. It didn't before.'

'Before, Alick.' The conjuror peered into the left-hand tunnel, his words distant. 'Since the Fidchell began, "before" is another world. Which way, Tod?'

The Tod-lowery pushed past Alick and snuffled down the tunnel entrances. 'The left is water,' he said at last. 'The right, fire.'

Tam Lin tapped the spear on a stone. 'Fire, for me.'

'No.' Luke said. 'We can't go through fire. And we must stay together.'

The pale face moved closer to the conjuror. 'You know I cannot touch the water.'

'Then you must pass over it,' Luke answered, as if he was laughing.

Something happened. Something rustled and flapped.

Then the Tod moved to where Tam Lin had been and picked up the fallen spear. A white bird sat on Luke's shoulder, preening. It sent a delicate downy feather into the darkness.

'If water is the worst thing down here,' the conjuror remarked, edging into the tunnel, 'we'll be very lucky.'

At first, the water was enough. It began after only a few steps. Alick's gloves were so wet he had taken them off, and now he could feel the walls turning slimy, and the cold trickle of moisture froze the ends of his fingers. Then his feet began to stick, squelching as he tugged them free. Something cold lapped about his wellingtons.

Grimly they trudged on, splashing downhill. The noise of the stream grew to fill the cavern, and after a while the first wave came over the top of Alick's boots and ran down in an icy cascade into his socks. He groaned.

'What's the matter?' the Tod laughed. 'Cold feet?'

Gritting his teeth, Alick watched the bird take off from Luke's shoulder and fly down the tunnel. Suddenly he realized he was seeing Luke more clearly than before; a faint light was growing ahead, and the conjuror was wading towards it. Just before it flew round the bend of the rock, the bird shone.

'We're coming out,' Luke shouted over his shoulder.

'Out where?' Alick murmured.

'Just about where we are now,' the Tod said. 'And where we have been since we came through that door.'

Alick frowned 'What?'

'Walking and standing still, my lad. They're all the same in the hollow hill.'

Trying to make sense of that, Alick waded round a rock, and stared, astonished.

Before him the stream cascaded out of the mouth of a cave and down a steep, rocky hillside. Below them a network of fields lay white with untrodden snow, and beyond those, a threatening fringe of dark pine forests stretched into the distance. The sky was iron-grey; every tree and hedgerow laden with snow, thick and heavy. A bitter wind whistled into their faces.

Alick shivered. 'It's not possible.'

'No,' said the Tod, splashing past.

'But where are we?'

'I told you. We're not anywhere — or anywhere you could put a name on.' The red paw grabbed his arm. 'Now then. Look at that!'

On the white field stood two pavilions, about a hundred yards apart, their doors facing. Each had a pennant flying from its roof; Alick could just make out the devices. On the black pavilion, a raven, and on the gold, a knight. And

87

between the two tents, facing him on a rocky knoll of its own, a great fortress, iron-grey, its gates wide open.

No one moved in the fields or the pavilions, or on the battlements of the fortress. The windows were staring blanks. Everything seemed deserted. Far over the woods one white bird circled.

Luke was sitting on a rock emptying water from his boots. The Tod scrambled down beside him, out of the wind. Alick followed. He took off his scarf and rubbed his numbed feet, then put the wet socks back on. He could never get wetter or colder than this.

The Tod sniffed. 'Looks deserted.'

'Good. Still, nothing here is as it seems.' Luke stared down at the castle with a smile. Alick tried another question.

'Are we still inside the Tump . . . I mean, is all this inside?'

The conjuror shook his head. 'I suggest you try not to think about it.'

'He means he doesn't know,' the Tod put in.

'Do you?' Luke said.

'Nope. Come on.'

They scrambled down the hill, over rocks and scree, and when they reached the bottom the wind snatched their breath and froze their faces. Alick pulled his hood on; Luke clutched his collar. Only the Tod seemed not to care about the cold. They plunged across the snowy waste, heads bent, struggling forward. Above, the white bird circled.

The field seemed enormous. However far they trudged, the great gates of the fortress came no nearer, and to each side the pavilions swayed and flapped in the icy wind.

It was eerie walking between them. Once, Alick paused and stared at the flapping draperies of the black tent. For a second the whole billowing structure seemed a vast black bird, struggling and flapping in the snow. Then the Tod tugged his arm, and he turned to face the fortress. It was still a long way off.

'I keep thinking,' he said, 'They might come out at us from these tents.'

Luke took no notice. He stopped and listened. A low sound, barely heard, troubled them.

'Thunder,' the Tod said.

'Bees?' Alick tried.

Luke shrugged. 'I don't think so.' He began to walk faster, taking some powder from a box in his pocket and sowing it liberally before his feet.

Instantly, the fortress was nearer. In a few steps they had reached the gates.

14

The Players

The gates were wide open. Pure untrodden snow filled the courtyard. Luke paused, and Alick noticed that he and the Tod were looking anxiously along the rows of dark, empty windows. The quiet was broken only by the wind, whistling through the bare cloisters, banging a door somewhere, sweeping dry snow into corners.

'Do we go in?'

Luke nodded. 'It'll be in here somewhere. Is the tree safe?'

Alick put his hand up and touched the small lump inside his coat. 'Yes.'

Tod was looking into a doorway. 'Start here. I'll feel better out of the open.'

As he said it, Alick gasped. 'Look!'

In the faint light the white gates were closing, swinging silently together. Snow jerked from them.

'It's best to be safe,' Luke said, hands in pockets. He

grinned at Alick. 'Don't want Them coming up behind us, do you?'

'No . . . Will it do any good?'

The Tod snorted, and Luke did not answer. Alick followed them up the stone steps. It was best not to be surprised at anything any more. Just shut up and tag along.

The steps were broken and dangerous. They wound upwards, past arrow slits that showed deserted courtyards below, and gardens of black, stunted trees. When they came to a corridor they walked down it in silence, and Luke flung open each door as they passed, but found only dusty, empty rooms, with broken windows and snow on the floorboards. No living thing — not a spider, not even an ant. Only, in the last room of all, a small silver fruit, rolling in the draught.

Alick picked it up. 'It's the same as the one I ate in the Tump.' He showed it to Luke. 'Are we near it, the Fidchell board?'

'Near enough!' Luke muttered.

Suddenly he glanced towards the window, so swiftly that Alick looked too, and saw a fire burning before each pavilion, blazing eerily in the snow.

'They weren't there before.'

The Tod was hustling him out of the room. 'We must find the board,' he said to Luke. 'It must be here.'

Luke bit his lip. 'Oh yes, but would we know it if we saw it?' They walked along corridors and up and down countless stairs, through many empty echoing halls. There was no sign of the chequered board, the table, the hall with its central fire. Then at one turn in a corridor a white bird sailed in through a window and became Tam Lin tapping Luke on the shoulder.

'They've reached the gates.'

91

As he spoke, a heavy thud shook the slabs of the floor under their feet, rumbling away into silence. And then came shouts, the far-off clash of metal. 'Didn't take them long,' the Tod sighed.

Alick was playing with the fruit in his pocket. Quietly, he took it out and put it in his mouth. After all, the first time . . .

The taste was as unpleasant as before. He felt suddenly sick and leaned against a window; a small dirty glass pane, only as big as a book. His eyesight swam, then steadied, and he saw . . . the Fidchell board!

'Look! Down there! What does that remind you of?'

Luke squeezed in beside him. Alick felt his body stiffen. Below them was a small courtyard, paved with black marble slabs. The dust of dead leaves lay on it, but not scattered randomly — it lay in a pattern; a pattern of black and gold squares. Leaves, and no tree.

'How do we get down there?' the Tod snapped. 'There must be a door.'

They clattered down some steps, Alick last, still feeling strange and dizzy. In front of him, the others faded, their voices indistinct. Above, heavy footsteps paced the corridors.

Then Alick saw it, the small door, shimmering in the wall. He pushed it, stepped through, and heard it click behind him.

He was a figure on a black and golden board. It stretched to the horizon in every direction, flat and unending. And he was alone on it; one solitary figure under a grey sky. Somewhere was the centre, the important square. How could he find it? It would look just the same as any other. He began to walk, and the wind swept across the empty acres and snatched his breath.

Suddenly, he turned. Around him the Fidchell pieces

were springing from the earth. Black and gold, glittering —
bird and horseman, greyhound, minstrel — as he had first
seen them at Talley, worlds and centuries ago. But this time
they were the giants, and he was tiny, tiny as an ant on a
chequered tablecloth. They towered above him, bestriding
their squares, eyes fixed on him. All around him. He was in
the middle, in the very centre.

For a moment, Alick hardly realized what that meant.
Then, as they began to move, to press closer, to clink and
rustle and flap towards him, he tugged the tree from his
pocket and ran across the huge blackness of the square
towards its centre, the very hub and axis of the great
spinning board. Breathless, he felt the black and gold giants
crush down on him. He held the tree, its leaves tinkled, a
shiver and roar swept the falling darkness. But before they
crashed over him he was kneeling, falling, and the roots of
the tree touched the black icy soil.

It exploded. It shot upwards and arched over him. Huge
and glittering, it erupted into leaf and branch like a firework
of jet and gold. Leaves and snow and dust cascaded on his
upturned face; leaves that rattled like tin in the sudden wind
and uprush, whirling round a great tree, heavy with fruit and
stars and birds, its branches tangling in the sky. The ground
heaved and buckled; twisting boles and roots snaked around
him; a cascade of leaves brushed and smothered his face and
became a curtain of gold that he reached out to, and
grabbed, and tugged firmly aside.

The Fidchell hall was quiet, and flooded with sunlight. Two
men were sitting at the table. One leaned back in his chair,
face towards Alick. The other was frowning at the board,
chin on hands. A dog lay asleep under the table, and a raven

on a gold chain croaked and hopped on the back of one of the chairs.

'So,' said the sprawling man to Alick, 'you're back.' The other looked up, interested. Neither seemed in the least surprised.

Alick stepped forward, and saw the tree on the centre square, exactly between the opposing armies. They all surveyed it, calmly.

The player with the raven sighed. 'It was not a long battle.'

'But some of the moves were interesting,' added the other. He glanced at Alick. 'Don't you think so?' He wore a fine fillet of gold in his hair.

Alick nodded, wary. He rubbed dust and leaves from his coat. 'Where are my friends?'

The players smiled at each other. 'They'll be here,' one said. 'The tree is back, so all the danger is ended.'

'And is the game over?'

'The game goes on for ever, secretly, here with us. You let it spill out into the world. Now you have brought it back.'

The player with the raven stood up. 'And it's time you left.' Whistling to the sleepy dog he walked over and opened one of the three doors.

Impossible breezes blew in, warm and sweet. Bees hummed in strange flowers. Alick saw an orchard, heavy with blossom. A stream ran through it, bubbling over stones, its surface a cloud of dragonflies. A white road led over distant hills.

'Where is that?' he whispered. The players smiled at each other. 'Go and see,' one of them said. 'You know you'd like to. Or perhaps you might prefer this.' Taking Alick by the elbow, he pushed him to the second door. A rose garden, in full bloom. Behind it a house of glass, its roof thatched with bright birds' feathers.

Alick shook his head. 'Where are these places? They look so . . . familiar.'

'Countries of the mind. Your mind. They are whatever you want them to be.'

'And you. Who are you?'

He knew they were smiling over his head. 'Just the players. Watching the ways of the world.'

The third door was very close. He made a picture in his mind, then reached out his hand, turned the knob, and opened it.

The sea.

The sea thundered on rocks somewhere below. Just through the door was grass, short and coarse — the top of a cliff. Not far out to sea was an island, misty with cloud and seagulls. He took a step closer. He wanted to see the water crash and foam far below. He wanted to step through the door. The player was close behind him, a hand at his back. 'Go on. There's no harm. Just for a look.'

Suddenly Alick stopped. 'No. No. I don't think so.' He turned quickly away.

'You're wise, Alick.' Luke was leaning just inside the curtain, his coat dark with water and dust. 'Don't go in.'

The players exchanged glances. 'He's seen us,' one said. 'He's seen the inside of the hill. You know . . .'

'I know,' Luke interrupted. 'But you can leave that to me. He will never find his way back in here, and if he should tell anyone of this, who would believe him?'

'Are you certain, sorcerer?'

'Quite certain.'

Alick came back and gazed down at the board. 'And if I had,' he said, 'what would have happened?'

'You know, don't you?' Luke moved aside for the Tod and the white dog. 'Nothing. You would walk to the edge of the cliff, gaze out to sea, come back. Just five minutes. But when you went back down into Halcombe you would have been away two hundred years.'

As they walked to the curtain, Alick paused and looked back. The players sat on their carven chairs, the dog asleep, the raven preening its feathers. Between them the Fidchell board gleamed, its knights and birds and ladies still and cold.

'Goodbye, Alick,' one of them said.

The other shook his head. 'He should have gone through the door, as all the others did.'

'All those tales,' the Tod said slyly as they walked down the tunnel, 'of those people who went into the wood and never came out.'

'You'll never have the chance again,' Luke added.

'What about you?'

The conjuror laughed. 'That's my business — which you are going to stay out of, from now on.'

At the entrance to the hollow, they paused. The door was wide open, the golden glow lighting falling flakes of snow. As Alick looked back down the tunnel the golden pillars stretched into the distance.

'I'll never understand all this.'

The door closed.

'Well,' the Tod grinned, 'the sun's coming. Until next time, sorcerer. And you, young one, I'll watch out for you in the wood. You're the sort that makes trouble, and no mistake.'

With a wink and a wave of its arm it was gone.

Alick and Luke walked slowly home through the wood. The white dog — or whatever it was — trotted along behind them, nosing roots and rabbit holes, just like any other dog. Light grew slowly; the first birds began to sing. Once past the Cross the going was easier; a gritting lorry had been along, strewing bright red gravel. As they came near to Halcombe the church clock chimed six.

'I'm going to catch it now,' Alick muttered.

'I doubt it.' Luke took his hands out of his pockets and blew on them. 'Your father could never have got home.'

'He could have phoned.'

'The lines were down.'

Alick thought about that. 'Good.'

'But he'll be home today. The blizzards are over.'

'Are you sure?'

Luke laughed. 'Quite sure. And Alick . . . don't follow me anywhere again.'

Alick grinned.

'And keep away from the Greenmere, unless you want more warts. Merry Christmas.'

'Merry Christmas, Luke.'

At the bookshop the key was on the ledge over the door. Alick thundered upstairs, turned on all the electric fires and sat in a huddle, shivering and tugging off wet clothes. Then he put the kettle on and went to the telephone.

'Jamie . . .? Yes, I know that's the time . . . Listen. Do you think your mother will make a pair of gloves for me, by Christmas? I know it's tomorrow! But listen, idiot, they're a bit special. They've got to have six fingers. Yes, that's what I said. Six.'

Other great reads *from* **Red Fox**

Further Red Fox titles that you might enjoy reading are listed on the following pages. They are available in bookshops or they can be ordered directly from us.

If you would like to order books, please send this form and the money due to:

ARROW BOOKS, BOOKSERVICE BY POST, PO BOX 29, DOUGLAS, ISLE OF MAN, BRITISH ISLES. Please enclose a cheque or postal order made out to Arrow Books Ltd for the amount due, plus 30p per book for postage and packing to a maximum of £3.00, both for orders within the UK. For customers outside the UK, please allow 35p per book.

NAME _____

ADDRESS _____

_____

Please print clearly.

Whilst every effort is made to keep prices low, it is sometimes necessary to increase cover prices at short notice. If you are ordering books by post, to save delay it is advisable to phone to confirm the correct price. The number to ring is THE SALES DEPARTMENT 071 (if outside London) 973 9700.

Other great reads from **Red Fox**

THE WINTER VISITOR   Joan Lingard

Strangers didn't come to Nick Murray's home town in winter.
And they didn't lodge at his house. But Ed Black had—and Nick
Murray didn't like it.

Why had Ed come? The small Scottish seaside resort was
bleak, cold and grey at that time of year. The answer, Nick
begins to suspect, lies with his mother—was there some past
connection between her and Ed?

ISBN 0 09 938590 2   £1.99

STRANGERS IN THE HOUSE   Joan Lingard

Calum resents his mother remarrying. He doesn't want to move
to a flat in Edinburgh with a new father and a thirteen-year-old
stepsister. Stella, too, dreads the new marriage. Used to living
alone with her father she loathes the idea of sharing their small
flat.

Stella's and Calum's struggles to adapt to a new life, while
trying to cope with the problems of growing up are related with
great poignancy in a book which will be enjoyed by all older
readers.

ISBN 0 09 955020 2   £2.99

Other great reads ⌇*from* **Red Fox**

Fantasy fiction—the Song of the Lioness series

ALANNA—THE FIRST ADVENTURE
Tamora Pierce

Alanna has just one wish—to become a knight. Her twin brother, Thom, prefers magic and wants to be a great sorcerer. So they swop places and Alanna, dressed as a boy, sets off for the king's court. Becoming a knight is difficult—but Alanna is brave and determined to succeed. And her gift for magic is to prove essential to her survival . . .

ISBN 0 09 943560 8   £3.50

IN THE HAND OF THE GODDESS
Tamora Pierce

Alan of Trebond is the smallest but toughest of the squires at court. Only Prince Jonathan knows she is really a girl called Alanna.

As she prepares for her final training to become a knight, Alanna is troubled. Is she the only one to sense the evil in Duke Roger? Does no one realise what a threat his steely ambition poses?

Alanna must use every ounce of her warrior skills and her gift for magic if she is to survive her Ordeal of Knighthood—and outwit the dangerous sorcerer duke.

ISBN 0 09 955560 3   £3.50

The third and fourth titles in the Song of the Lioness series, THE GIRL WHO RODE LIKE A MAN and LIONESS RAMPANT will be published by Red Fox in July 1992.

Other great reads from **Red Fox**

**Haunting fiction for older readers from
Red Fox**

THE XANADU MANUSCRIPT
John Rowe Townsend

There is nothing unusual about visitors in Cambridge.

So what is it about three tall strangers which fills John with
a mixture of curiosity and unease? Not only are they strikingly
handsome but, for apparently educated people, they are oddly
surprised and excited by normal, everyday events. And, as John
pursues them, their mystery only seems to deepen.

Set against a background of an old university town, this
powerfully compelling story is both utterly fantastic and oddly
convincing.

'An author from whom much is expected and received.'
Economist

ISBN 0 09 975180 1   £2.99

ONLOOKER   Roger Davenport

Peter has always enjoyed being in Culver Wood, and dismissed
the tales of hauntings, witchcraft and superstitions associated
with it. But when he starts having extraordinary visions that
are somehow connected with the wood, and which become more
real to him than his everyday life, he realizes that something
is taking control of his mind in an inexplicable and frightening
way.

Through his uneasy relationship with Isobel and her father,
a Professor of Archaeology interested in excavating Culver
Wood, Peter is led to the discovery of the wood's secret and
his own terrifying part in it.

ISBN 0 09 975070 8   £2.99

Other great reads from **Red Fox**

THE WINTER VISITOR   Joan Lingard

Strangers didn't come to Nick Murray's home town in winter. And they didn't lodge at his house. But Ed Black had—and Nick Murray didn't like it.

Why had Ed come? The small Scottish seaside resort was bleak, cold and grey at that time of year. The answer, Nick begins to suspect, lies with his mother—was there some past connection between her and Ed?

ISBN 0 09 938590 2   £1.99

STRANGERS IN THE HOUSE   Joan Lingard

Calum resents his mother remarrying. He doesn't want to move to a flat in Edinburgh with a new father and a thirteen-year-old stepsister. Stella, too, dreads the new marriage. Used to living alone with her father she loathes the idea of sharing their small flat.

Stella's and Calum's struggles to adapt to a new life, while trying to cope with the problems of growing up are related with great poignancy in a book which will be enjoyed by all older readers.

ISBN 0 09 955020 2   £2.99